MORRISON'S FRIEND

MORRISON'S FRIEND

A Novel

Ignacio L. Götz

Strategic Book Publishing and Rights Co.

Strategic Book Publishing and Rights Co., LLC
USA | Singapore
www.sbpra.com

For information about special discounts for bulk purchases please contact Strategic Book Publishing and Rights Co. Special Sales at bookorder@sbpra.net.

ISBN: 978-1-68181-538-1

Nothing justifies one's existence like being loved.

Goethe

CHAPTER ONE

He was sitting comfortably in an over-stuffed leather chair in the lobby of the Marriott, waiting for the bishop to arrive. The e-mail message he had received was terse and clear: "Meet me at the Long Island Marriott on the 30th. Very important. Bishop Reilly." He had called the bishop's office, but the secretary had been evasive, insisting that the bishop could not speak to him until their meeting on the 30th.

When he had arrived at the Marriott, he had asked at the front desk if there were any messages for Mr. Jones, James Jones, but there were none. So now he waited.

He hadn't seen the Bishop for years, not since his late teens when they had been together in seminary. They had formed a close friendship then, maintaining it over the years through correspondence and phone calls. They didn't live too far from each other, but their lives had diverged, and professional commitments made it difficult to socialize. Of course, it was possible to meet, to go out for dinner, or take a stroll along the beach, but it was not necessary. Trusting their feelings for each other, they knew that their friendship was secure. They felt at ease with each other whenever they spoke, and their letters were always newsy and affectionate.

John—for that was the Bishop's name—had risen quickly in the hierarchy. After serving in a parish for a few years, he had been transferred to the Chancery, where he displayed unusual administrative talent. It had been a foregone conclusion that he would be elevated to a bishopric, and so his consecration came as a surprise to no one. Jones had been invited to the ceremony, but was unable to attend.

Still, their friendship had continued. The pomp and circumstance surrounding the bishop's life had not altered that. And yet, the message had caught Jones by surprise. What could be so important and pressing that the Bishop had to request his presence? Why couldn't he have written or phoned? He had just looked at his watch one more time when he spied the bishop ambling into the lobby.

"So wonderful to see you, John," he said, hugging him without inhibition. The bishop stooped a bit, he noticed, and his hair was grayer than he had imagined it would be. He looked older than his mid-fifties, but he still seemed fit.

"Jim, old friend, how are you?" the bishop queried with the same old, twangy Irish accent of his youth. "You look so fresh and healthy. How come the city smog doesn't wilt you a bit, you old bush?"

"You forget I live mostly indoors," he replied, holding the bishop at arm's length, looking cheerily into his eyes. "I am a potted plant, you know."

"Potted, my foot," the bishop laughed. "A plastic plant, I'd say, like the greenery at McDonald's."

"I bet you never thought it'd come to this, that you'd be caught talking to a plastic bush!"

They both laughed as they walked, arm in arm, to one of the ample sofas in the lobby. Sitting down, they exchanged more pleasantries about their respective appearances. Presently, the bishop said, "I'm sure you were surprised when you received my message."

"Indeed," Jones replied, "not just at the urgency, but because you wouldn't answer my phone calls. You've never been this secretive before. What the heck is going on?"

"Well, Jim," the bishop said as he lowered his voice. He looked around briefly to see whether or not he could be overheard. "It's a matter that closely concerns the Diocese. But we can't let it be known that we are concerned. That's why I wouldn't talk to you on the phone. I can't even trust my own secretary."

"You're exaggerating, I'm sure," Jones said, though exaggeration was not one of the bishop's faults.

"Well, judge for yourself. Here's the scoop."

The bishop looked around again for eavesdroppers, but he seemed satisfied. People were going about their business without paying any attention to them, and no one else was seated in the lobby.

"Do you remember Morrison, the poet? Died about twenty-five years ago?"

"Vaguely," said Jones. "I remember him as a minor poet, but I don't recall reading any of his stuff. There was some fuss about something toward the end of his life, if I remember correctly, but that's about it."

"That's the man," said the bishop, "and your memory still serves you well. You got the main details"

"So, what's the matter with him?"

"Well, you see," the bishop explained as he leaned forward to get closer to Jones, "Morrison had been baptized and raised Catholic. He didn't practice for most of his life, but he was a deeply religious man. His poetry shows him that way, even his less edifying stuff, you know, sex poems and the like. He seems to have had this mystical streak in him that surfaced in his writings and his lectures."

He stopped momentarily and looked around again. "He had a following," the bishop continued, as he lowered his voice even more. "You know how it is—people think that because you are a mystic, you've got the key to the treasure chest of happiness, or of heaven, or whatever. People will follow anyone who seems to hold out to them the promise of salvation because he knows *the path*. That seems to have been the case with Morrison."

"What has this got to do with the price of eggs in Hong Kong?" asked Jones.

"Many thought Morrison was a saint. It's hard to know how many, but after Morrison's death we began to get letters from all over the world requesting that some inquiry be made into the possibility of declaring him a saint."

"People still go for that kind of thing?" Jones asked. The bishop raised his finger as if to admonish him, but Jones shot back, "Wait! Wait! I was joking. No sermons, please." The bishop leaned back, smiling.

"But seriously," Jones added, "I don't understand why this kind of thing is still going on. Isn't it enough to live with the holiness of a person, to treasure the inner experience and the words of wisdom, without needing official declarations and cults?"

"I wish it were so, Jim," responded the bishop, "I wish it were so. But we are still as caught in the mire of official pronouncements and legitimations as we were eight-hundred years ago. It's a power play, I guess, and it seems to satisfy an urge among the people, a hunger for authentication. The pope could float another sale of indulgences today, and people would still buy them and flock to theologians for verification of the terms. And another Luther would still rise to question the legitimacy of the promises. We are a strange lot, we are."

"I understand," Jones observed, "but this Morrison character—"

"We want to be prepared," the bishop interrupted. "I don't think it will go anywhere, this talk of sainthood, but I'd rather not wait until pressure builds and demands make matters more difficult. You see . . . we want to find out for sure if Morrison was really a saint. We want to know this before any inquiry begins—if one ever begins at all."

"Okay," said Jones.

"There's more," the bishop continued. "The biographies that appeared after Morrison's death detail an episode in his life, something to do with sexual harassment. I didn't know Morrison personally, but from what I have learned, the charge would have been ludicrous. Morrison doesn't seem to have been that sort of person. But the biographies did mention the charge, and that led to some apprehension in the minds of many about his alleged sanctity. Then, a collection that was published posthumously, contained poems supposedly connected with the sexual harassment charge."

"I see," said Jones.

"The publication of the poems started a small controversy—really, a tempest in a teapot, but, still a tempest. And yet, the belief in Morrison's holiness remains unabated. Some disillusionment with him has appeared in certain quarters, but overall, his fame has grown, if anything."

The bishop paused for a moment, again looking around furtively. "We can't remain in limbo as far as Morrison's sanctity is concerned. We must be certain, one way or the other. Frankly, I have no stake in the matter, but it is my responsibility to make sure that the truth about Morrison is ascertained."

"And you want my advice in the matter?" Jones asked.

"Yes, in a manner of speaking. But actually, I want more from you. I want you to find out the truth about Morrison. Of course, that includes the truth about the charge of sexual harassment, but it is not restricted to that. You must get hold of Morrison's life—his entire life—and weigh all the major factors and events in it. Then you must make a recommendation to me. If it ever comes to pass that we have to decide on initiating an inquest into Morrison's sanctity, I want to be ready to answer Yes or No, and for that, I must know the truth, the truth about Morrison."

"On what grounds do people say he was a saint?"

"Besides the mystical poetry, you mean?" asked the bishop.

Jones nodded affirmatively.

"Well," the bishop explained, "for one thing, he was a very compassionate man. Not just with his students—that's to be expected—but he and his wife would spend the summers working at various Indian reservations or doing relief work in flooded areas of the Midwest, and on a couple of occasions even in Bangladesh. You know, this kind of thing takes more commitment than making charitable contributions."

"I see," Jones said again.

"Did you know he taught at Rikers Island for years?" the bishop asked, spying Jones's reaction. "To inmates," he added with emphasis, "weekend after weekend, and he would even get some of their poems published. Of course, some people claimed he'd changed their lives, that he worked miracles with the young."

Jones looked at the bishop, expecting more.

"That's all I know, Jim," Bishop Reilly said. "After all, it's you who's supposed to get the load on Morrison!"

"But why me?" said Jones. "Why are you picking me to do this dirty job for you? It is a dirty job, you understand."

"Jim, we have known each other for some forty years. You are my best friend. You know that. I have absolute confidence in you, not only in your discretion—can you imagine what would happen if your search were discovered—but also in your judgment. I trust your judgment. And I think that, given your past experience and studies in seminary, you will have the religious sensitivity to investigate this matter and arrive at a sound and justifiable recommendation."

Jones shifted his weight in the chair, pondering the pros and cons of the task, looking for words to express the many thoughts and feelings, misgivings and interests, reluctance and attraction, that were coursing through his mind in response to the bishop's request.

"Some friend you are," he said finally.

The bishop smiled. "I know I'm asking a lot, my friend, but I also know you are capable of giving a lot. By the way, we will cover all your expenses. I will get you your own private account number, and all bills will be paid from it. I can even pay you a salary."

"That won't be necessary," said Jones. "I couldn't do this for money. If I do it—and I haven't said I will—it will be solely a matter of friendship. A thing between two people who have loved each other for some forty years, as you said."

He wondered what it meant to call—or be called by—someone *best friend*. He pondered this in the background of his mind, while the topic of conversation stayed in the foreground, like a subsidiary melody playing beneath the symphony's main theme. Was friendship a matter of doing or feeling? Were there things one did for a best friend that one would not do for others? Perhaps. But he thought it was also about emotions. Surely a best friend evokes a range of feelings by his very presence or even a remembrance of him. Perhaps it was a question of caring, of loving another without knowing how or why. Could there be limits to this love, and what might they be?

"You know, John," he finally said, "no one has called me his best friend until you did just now. I hope you weren't saying that merely to lure me into this mess of a job."

"Jim," said the bishop, "I wouldn't lie to you. Feelings of love are strange; they are difficult to sort out, and perhaps more so in friendship than in any other type of relationship." He paused, as if to take stock of the situation. Continuing, he looked Jones straight in the eye, "Jim, you have always been my best friend, but I haven't been mature enough to tell you. There is always a lurking fear that friendships will be misunderstood, as if a really true thing between two people were too rare to be normal."

"I know," said Jones, pleased, though somewhat embarrassed. John had always been his dearest friend, but he wondered if he had ever told him so. "Have I ever told you that *you* are my best friend, too?"

"No," said the bishop, "but I am glad you said it. Being a priest is a lonely thing, Jim, a very lonely thing. Our friendship, unstated as it has been for years, has been a great support. You are the only witness I have of my humanity, of the fact that I can love as ordinary people do."

They were both silent for a time, relishing their friendship, remembering past exchanges, wondering about the future.

"You know," the bishop said after a while, "perhaps my interest in Morrison's truth is tied up with my interest in my own. What kind of a man am I, Jim? Am I a saint, too?"

"You are not dead yet," Jones responded with a smile. "Relax."

"I know I should." A minute passed before he added, "Let's do something for friendship's sake, something we haven't done for years. Let's go for a swim. I have a membership here at the spa. And then let's ride to Jones Beach and walk barefoot on the sand."

"Yes," said Jones, "let's do that."

CHAPTER TWO

Jones decided that the first order of business was to read about Morrison, to get a sense of the man. He walked to Brentano's but found that the main biography of Morrison, *A Poet's Life*, had been out of print for quite some time. There were several other books that chronicled literary and business friendships, but the two that included Morrison were also out of print. The *Elegies* was out of print as well, but he was able to buy a large volume that contained Morrison's collected poetry.

From Brentano's, he walked to the public library at 40th Street, and there he found the books he was after. He took out *A Poet's Life*, ensconced himself comfortably in the main reading room, and started reading.

According to the author, Morrison was born in 1922, in New York City—the Bronx, to be precise. His parents were lower middle class, and they had lived in several apartments between the Grand Concourse and the Rose Hill section. Morrison attended Roosevelt High School, opposite Fordham University, and would often roam alone, in meditative moods, through the undulating lawns of the campus.

He had still been a teenager when the Japanese bombed Pearl Harbor, and he joined the Navy in the wake of the attack. He had seen action in the Pacific, and was discharged at the end of the war. Thanks to the GI Bill, he was able to attend college at Fordham, where he majored in English. Upon graduation in 1950, he started teaching English at his old high school. And by attending classes summer after summer, he slowly earned a Master's degree in creative writing from New York University. His first poems had appeared here and there during the early 1950s, but it was not till the 1960s that the first collections of his work were published. He married Ann Collins in 1948, and they had three children during the 1950s. He continued teaching at Roosevelt High School until his retirement in 1987, and he and Ann continued to live in their spacious Grand Concourse apartment until his death in 1992. That was, essentially, the outline of his life.

There was nothing extraordinary here. In fact, Morrison appeared to have lived a very ordinary life. His time had been devoted entirely to his family, his teaching, and his writing. He had been a devoted husband and father, taking a lively interest in the lives of his three sons, all of whom had attended college and gotten married, and now were leading their own separate lives in different parts of the country. He and Ann had traveled some, mostly within the continental United States, with a couple of trips to Canada and the British Virgin Islands. His salary as a teacher, and the income from his books and an occasional lecture tour, did not support extravagances. Still, their lives were far from dull, for they jointly enjoyed the adventure of ideas.

Morrison had enjoyed a reputation as an excellent teacher and been effective right up to the time of his retirement. Perhaps the most distinctive thing about his teaching was that he could convey to his students the excitement he felt for literature as the fruit of the human imagination. The delight he felt for words—for what they conjured up in the mind, for how poets grouped them for effect—was something he brought constantly to his students, who generally became infected by the same exhilaration.

His tendency was to wax lyrical, to get caught up in the excitement of the vision, of the experience, and let his emotions gush forth, often in beautiful language. But, usually this kind of writing was too limpid, the language too direct. Such poems could be unidimensional, bordering on superficiality, like a Chopin waltz. But in his best poetry, the mystery he was elucidating was that of human feeling. To evoke this kind of mystery, he had to hone his verse, making it highly metaphorical and compact. These poems approached more closely the essence of poetry as craft. They represented a determined and studied effort to reveal the secrets of the world without destroying the mystery. His output fluctuated between these two poles, although the second one was more representative of his later work.

An exception—wrote the author of *A Poet's Life*—was the *Elegies*, which combined lyrical poems with thoroughly crafted ones, whose meaning required slow and painstaking exploration.

A Poet's Life did not devote much space to Morrison's "affair," which had given rise to the *Elegies*. Apparently, as part of promotional activities, Morrison would participate in talk shows, either alone or with other poets, novelists, and artists. It was on one of these shows that he had met a young, aspiring actress who was striving to make a career in Hollywood. A friendship developed—spontaneous, warm, reassuring—that was renewed sporadically at similar promotional affairs. It led Morrison to write the *Elegies*, but when he showed the young actress drafts of the early poems, she felt threatened by their sexual nature and put a stop to the friendship, at least for a time. The other books that chronicled the friendship went into slightly greater detail, but still without making much of the affair. All of the books refused to divulge the name of the actress or any details that might lead to her being identified.

It was not the biographers who had magnified the affair or implied that the matter was scandalous. That had simply happened as Morrison's devotees read the accounts after his death and perceived them as possible stains on his saintly character. From what Jones could gather, all three accounts had been researched and, for the most part, written while Morrison was still alive. But they had not been published until two or three years after his death. By that time, no further evidence could be obtained from him. Ann, Morrison's wife, seemed to know nothing of the matter, and the *Elegies* would not be published until 1996.

Thus, Jones was confronted with an essentially simple, ordinary life, marked by devotion to duty. The matter of holiness, which the biographers didn't even mention, had simply grown from a combination of respect for this devotion to duty and the mystical strains of Morrison's published poetry. Ordinary people, not scholars or biographers, had made the synthesis. But while Jones could find no singular grounds for pronouncing Morrison a saint, he couldn't, either, conceive of proof against his holiness. Morrison's life was simply *his* life. There were no major milestones, no startling episodes, and no extraordinary achievements. He would have to look further.

CHAPTER THREE

Jones decided to take a look at Morrison's poetry. There was a thick volume of collected verse that encompassed several small tomes previously published separately; then there was the slim pamphlet of the *Summer Elegies*. He thought he ought to look first for poems which in some way revealed Morrison's mystical vein. After all, these were the inspiration for his cult following. The poems were not hard to find. From his earliest published work until his later years, the transcendental sense was clear and unequivocal—no wonder people had picked up the scent. In the fifties, he was already writing about the divine, in search of his soul:

> . . . to the huge chaotic maelstrom falling
> He sought me, found me, loved me;
> I knew Him not,
> and sensing but that misty darkness, ill-foreboding,
> I struggled, fought, revolted . . .
> He did not strike, nor shoe, forsake, or lower,
> nor freed He me, O that tremendous lover.

At times the poems spoke of Morrison's own search for the Divine Presence, hidden, though eventually discovered, in the ordinary realities of life. Again, in a poem from the fifties, he could write:

> Where were then Thou?
> What luring snare
> had trapped me there,
> Thy radiant glare
> preventing me to share?
>
> But Thou wert there
> amidst those clouds;
> Thy golden hair,
> Thy perfect mould,
> were moulded everywhere;
> that voicing loud,
> that cobalt pair . . .

This theme was repeated in many of the sonnets and also in later individual poems. One from the late fifties, "Sonnet XXIV," could be taken as representative:

> I looked into the rose, Thou wert not there,
> And yet its beauty pleased my searching eye;
> The rose-bush did not hide Thy mortal share,
> And yet its fragrance told me Thou wert by.

I walked amidst the lilies white and pure
And in their chaste beds gently searched for Thee;
I called Thy name so sweetly 'twas a lure,
Yet there again discovered I not Thee.
I chased a nightingale across the wood
With wistful hopes it would lead me to Thee;
Alack, but fly I could not, though I would,
And thus remained alone, my self with me.
My hopes dispelled, then, with a hopeless flair
I turned me to my self, and found Thee there.

This was mystical poetry in the tradition of the great visionaries of all ages. Rûmî could have written such a poem, or St. Augustine, whose passionate search for the divine beyond the grandeur of nature was captured by Morrison in "Sonnet XXXIV," part of which read:

Oft ye I questioned and weighed in my mind
The answers that ye gave; ye all scorned fame,
And asked if ye were God ye called me blind,
And thus of my sad query fanned the flame.
"We are not God, we are not God," ye said;
"Seek thou above, seek thou above"— and fled.

By the sixties, Morrison seemed to have found a way to step beyond the narrowness of the self and to open his soul to God:

. . . My narrowness is glass,
skin back to skin, front to back so close! No self
stands in the way! Transparent through my narrow self I look
and vast expanses open up before my eyes, the world
beaútiful in light ethereal . . .

By the seventies, his mystical sense had acquired feminine dimensions, prompted, probably, by his study of Indian mysticism and the work of Jung. A stanza of a poem from the late seventies illustrates this perfectly:

Sink, spirit, sink
into the Naught aquamarine,
translucent void;
thrust self,
live spindled wheel,
into the calyxed hub
where coddled axles whirl.

Re-live Er's vision
in the timeless cavern, sport
again inscrutably the smile
of Shakyamuni.

Discourse no more
with Nicodemus on rebirth:

Morrison's Friend

my
w
o
m
b

a
w
a
i
t
s

y
o
u

n
o
w

d
n
a

e
v
e
r
m
o
r
e
.
.
.
.

Clearly, Morrison had the makings of a mystical poet. Whether or not that was enough to make him a saint was quite another story. This was something he would have to fit with the rest of Morrison's life. Besides, there were still the sexual poems, and the *Elegies*. He turned to these next.

Many of the early sonnets dealt with friendship. There was nothing startling there, nothing that could make a puritan take offense. But by the sixties, poems with a decidedly sexual turn were beginning to appear. For example:

My hands explored your form
as if I had a diamond in my hands,
of them each pore an eye,
wide-open, wonder-struck.

And again:

Within my arms
that moan that stills a thousand sighs
within my heart.

A poem from the seventies was even more explicit:

Night came at last, and I relented,
half demented,

to the soft allurements of the dark.
I roamed the parks
enveloped by the wings of larks,
and laid in sylvan couches,
exchanged caresses, vouches,
tapping sap,
plugging gap,
sunk in Nature's orgiastic lap.

And in a poem titled "Summer Squall," the sexual content became more direct and personal:

I snugged warmly to your belly
for now your mood was changing,
your bosom heaved with stormy passion
as the summer squall approached us.
I sought your cave amidst convulsions,
hid my own turbulent emotion,
torrents oozed upon your ground,
thunderous groans resounded,
receded slowly, 'til
the parting gusts of gale
kept rhythm with the panting sighs
of our surfeiture.

There was nothing outrageous here, nothing scandalous. Morrison, after all, was married. It was reasonable to expect that at some time his poetry would deal with the sexual aspect of his life. But Jones could also understand how many would have had difficulty reconciling this kind of verse with the mystical poetry Morrison had written. Even though the mystics had often expressed their ecstasies in sexually explicit language, people had trouble integrating sexuality with the spiritual quest, as if the former were a blotch on the white, seamless tunic of the soul. In the West, ever since Gnostic times, sexuality had been reckoned as evil, because it was deemed to be material, and everything material was evil. Hadn't matter, after all, according to Persian doctrine, been created by Ahriman, the principle of evil? St. Paul, or whoever wrote those letters, had clearly preferred "spiritual" people over the "carnal," a major reason why sex had eventually been downgraded to a sin, with chastity and celibacy preferred. But how could creation itself be evil? This had been a major problem St. Augustine had faced as he tried to understand his own world. Hadn't God, the God of the Bible, created everything? And if he had created everything, then how could one call some things good and some things evil? Didn't the Bible say explicitly that God saw everything that he had created and called it all "good"? So where did evil originate? What was evil? St. Augustine had answered the question in his *Confessions*, and his answer had become standard. Jones knew the answer was different in the East, where there was even a cultic way to the divine that involved ritual intercourse. Some

Indian temples abounded with statues in postures that were, at least to the eyes of Westerners, erotic. Still, this was not India, and he had to deal with the values prevalent in his own culture.

* * *

At this point he decided to take a look at the *Elegies.* The unpretentious pamphlet lay on his desk, beckoning. Perhaps he would find there the missing clues to the interpretation of Morrison—perhaps not. At any rate, he wouldn't know until he read them. He picked up the booklet and read.

Summer Elegies

by

William Morrison

Edited by
Thomas Pickering

1996

INTRODUCTION

The *Summer Elegies*, published here posthumously, contain some of the finest poetry Morrison ever wrote. They are the product of his late years, and at least some of them bear a distinctive mark of maturity and depth, as well as of poetic diction. The manuscript was found among Morrison's papers, many of which were entrusted to me for review and editing by Morrison's wife, Ann.

The order in which the *Elegies* are being published is that in which they were found, but there seems to be a distinct chronology among them, building up to the concluding lines of "No. 5," borrowed from Shakespeare's *Hamlet*: "A consummation devoutly to be wish'd." These words, also, offer an important key to the interpretation of the poems, as will be explained presently.

"No. 5," however, does not mark the end of the *Elegies*. Nos. 6, 7, 8, and 9 are poems of self-examination and self-doubt, written, still, in the more direct style of the first five poems. After these, the style changes. It is as if the direct and passionate language of the first five *Elegies* were giving way to a more metaphorical, more profound diction. In the latter *Elegies*, Morrison's meaning must be gleaned from the pictures his words paint rather than from the language itself, as in the earlier poems. This, in a sense, renders them more interesting, since interpretation becomes necessary.

Morrison was, in many ways, a reserved man.[1] But he was generally jovial and spirited, and exuded a certain *joie de vivre* that was often infectious, and that he maintained even amidst adverse and depressing conditions. His marriage was a happy and fruitful one, and he was obviously proud of his progeny. His career was generally successful, and it brought him recognition and respect. Nevertheless, in his later years, Morrison had become impatient with himself. He felt still full of life, despite lacking the superabundant energy of his earlier years. And he began to see himself as somewhat shackled by societal restrictions against which he felt rebellious. To judge from the *Elegies*, especially "No. 8," he seems to have dreamed of starting life all over again. He loved his wife, but he fantasized about surviving her death and falling in love again with a young and beautiful woman, a companionable and intelligent one, with whom he could enjoy the resumed

1 The best biography of Morrison is D. M. Sundari, *A Poet's Life* (New York: Subscribers & Co., 1995), where the factual material mentioned here is explained at length. Other significant contributions are: Tamra Loremaci, *Business Friendships* (New York: MBA, 1994), and Douglas Freemantle, *Friendship Then, Then, and Now* (New York: Architectures, 1994).

adventures of love and sex, discovery and travel, and who would be a willing and loving partner. It appears that Morrison liked to fantasize, and that the *Elegies* are the fruit of fantasies surrounding his frustrations.[2] This context of love and fantasy is, it seems to me, the one in which the *Elegies* were written. Most of them were finished in the summer of 1987, hence the title. Their lyric quality, and the way they are spread over the pages, bears witness to a pent up force that finally gushed forth in poetry, because it would not find consummation in real life.

Though never published during his lifetime, the *Elegies* were central to an episode that affected Morrison profoundly. Morrison formed what he thought was a very close friendship with a young aspiring actress, a woman of great beauty, wit, and character, whom he met at a reception promoting one of his books.[3] They saw each other seldom, since she lived and worked in Los Angeles, and when they did, their meetings were chaste though fun-filled. It is not implausible to conclude that she is at least one of the women (if there were more than one) about whom Morrison fantasized in the *Elegies*.

---

2 Freemantle, 312; Sundari, 465ff., Loremaci, 230ff.

3 Morrison's biographers deliberately shield her identity: Sundari, 397; Lorecima, 233; Freemantle, 314.

At the beginning, their friendship was untrammeled. They exchanged thoughts, impressions, and recollections, with a freedom beautiful to behold. But Morrison seems to have read into her confidences (and into what he thought were innuendos) a greater love than she was prepared to give, though his affection for her remained innocent and pure. Thinking her love deeper and larger than it perhaps was, he offered her a friendship in which nothing was denied, not even his fantasies. As a result, he showed her early versions of some of the *Elegies*, which he had originally intended to be private, as is clear from his journal and from the fact that he didn't show them to his wife, Ann. The actress recognized herself as their subject, but misunderstood the fantasies for reality and concluded that the poems, and his showing them to her, was propositioning amounting to sexual harassment, though she assured him she would not press charges against him.

This accusation hurt Morrison deeply, for he was forever the champion of women's rights. He thought that his misconstrued behavior, perhaps objectively open to misunderstanding, had flowed out of the purest and most innocent of intentions and had taken place before someone he felt would be incapable of misunderstanding it.[4] However, it was indeed

4 Freemantle notes (314-15) that in the margin of page 1 of a draft of No. 11, there is a quotation from *Cat on a Hot Tin Roof*, Act II: "Any true thing between two

misunderstood, and the episode sadly ruined what he had hoped would be a lasting and beautiful friendship. As a result, one must surmise, his self-image was damaged, and he lost confidence in himself.

The distinction between his friendship and his fantasies had been clear to him: he really loved her as a friend, even though he fantasized about her as his lover. His mistake had been to think that because she cared for him, he could reveal to her his fantasies about her (and, perhaps, about other women). But she had mistakenly interpreted the revelation as a declaration of intent and, therefore, felt threatened and harassed.

This incident was very frustrating to Morrison, and very painful, but he felt there was nothing he could do but let time pass. Eventually, he wrote her a note which read, "If you are ever ready and willing, between now and eternity, to talk about what happened, I'd be very thankful." She received the note,[5] but it is not clear if a further conversation ever took place between them before Morrison's death.

This pain is captured, I think, in several of the poems, especially, "No. 9." Even though they were placed by Morrison toward the center of the *Elegies*, I believe they were composed later, after he had shown her the earlier, more sexual, poems, and her

people is too rare to be normal." The gloss is clearly a later addition.

5 Freemantle, 315; Lorecima, 233; Sundari, 397-98.

reaction had upset the flow of his fantasies. This is also the reason, I believe, why the later poems deal more with hope than with the realization of a fantasy.

To sum up, I am convinced that there was no actual affair, and that the *Elegies*, therefore, represent a kind of sublimation of a wished-for passion. The definitive confirmation of this comes from the words of "No. 5" already quoted: "A consummation/devoutly to be wish'd." Even though the phrase makes perfect sense within the logic of the poem, I think it is Morrison's way of hinting at the fantastic nature of his love. The words reappear in "No. 15" and in "No. 14," though slightly changed ("A consolation/devoutly to be wish'd"), and the meaning is similar: they express a wish for a reality that could only be fantasized.

Finally, a word must be said about "No. 15." It is a poem about hope written in the manner of T. S. Eliot's *The Waste Land*, though there is a prankishness to it foreign to the great classic. Each of the six sections of the poem takes up an aspect of hope and develops it in terms of events and/or personages from mythology and contemporary literature. The mixture is convincing, and, as a whole, the poem works.

In the appended Bibliography I have listed the works of authors from Morrison's library whom he most likely studied in the process of preparing this poem.

As for the text, there were no variant readings in the manuscript. The emendations—and there were many—seemed final, and, therefore, I have used them as Morrison's definitive choice of words. The footnotes contain material relevant to an understanding of the poems, and are clearly marked [Ed.].

BIBLIOGRAPHY

Ernst Bloch, *Man on his own.* (New York: Herder & Herder, 1970).

Douglas Freemantle, *Friendship Then, Then, and Now.* (New York: Architectures, Inc., 1994).

M. Esther Harding, *Woman's Mysteries.* (Boston: Shambhala, 1990).

Tamra Loremaci, *Business Friendships.* (New York: MBA Publishing House, Inc., 1994).

Gabriel Marcel, *Homo Viator.* (New York: Harper Torchbooks, 1962).

Gabriel García Márquez, *Love in the Time of Cholera.* (New York: Knopf, 1988).

Jürgen Moltmann, *Theology of Hope.* (New York: Harper & Row, 1967).

D. M. Sundari, *A Poet's Life.* (New York: Subscribers & Co., 1995).

SUMMER ELEGIES

No. 1

I loved you first as you,
and then, again, as you
and for a long time
you were the center of my thoughts,
the theme of dream and fancy—

yours the face
that closed my eyes in sleep
and lit my every morn;
the ghostly friend that talked
companioning my walks—

you
the doctor of my ills
dispensing from an ancient well
rejuvenating drink—

you
th' inspiring presence of my life;
you—

No. 2

I knew your needs
and the vastness of your soul,
how you were worthy to be loved,
and, ah! how much—
I knew how best to love you,
and that none could better do,

and that past self-deceit
I did not love my loving you
but you,
as no one ever could, or would—

I wanted so to love you
as you had never dreamed you could,
and as you should,
though you had doubted that you ever would.
And this itself
was grounds for loving you
much more
than anyone could dream to do.

No. 3

"He who lusts in his heart has sinned,"[6]
he said. "Sweet sin," I said, "if
the lust's for you."

And what of love
in the heart, and love for you?

The yearning burns uninterruptedly,
a slow, smoldering burn that yearns
never to cease to burn till the burning
cease; and how could it
when your beauty fans the flame?

"Nothing fairer in the world to see
than the union of a noble soul
and an outward form, its counterpart."[7]

6 *Matthew* 5:28. [Ed.]

7 Plato *Republic*, 402. [Ed.]

I sit by you, awed and aflame,
like Sappho, dumb, by Anactoria,
lost in a love-trance no one knows,
feigning professional respect,
and all the while

yearning to hold you close,
and yearning that the yearning never cease—

What torment,
wishing for the end of torment
but no end to love,
therefore wishing the denial of the wish—

What portent!
Sin turned to grace,
and you the potent alchemist.

No. 4

The point was pleasure,
Aphrodite's game:
to waken every sensuous cell
of your radiant, supple form,
the spongy tissues of your thighs,
the smooth contours of your chest
up to the very nipples of your breasts;
humming
the long cadenzas of your legs;
sinking
toward the luscious woodlands of your glen.
Climbing, then, panting,
my mouth against your virgin soil,
the rising, roving region
of your *Venusberg*;
devouring your mouth,

our tongues a Gordian knot;
and all the while,

the fingers fondling every inch
of languidly contorting body mass,
of thrusting hips;
and every limb retouched a thousand times—

until the well-known moan
signaled the pleasure's avalanche,
and bit by bit the heaving ceased,
and you relaxed, aglow,
the warmth of inner surfeit
tingling in your skin,
caressed still, in the fold
of my embrace.

No. 5

Virginal,
your body clung to mine
even as released
our passion's sighs
died in each other's lips,
slobbered, sucked,
the sensuous act complete;

and we, cemented,
never to be sundered-split,
till we succumbed, perhaps,
before the world's rebirth,
to be reborn entwined—
— a consummation
devoutly to be wish'd.

No. 6

Am I what I think I've grown to be,
what I have labored to become
decade after decade after birth:

not a flawless work of art,
a masterpiece,
but all in all an imitable shape,
by Nietzsche's reckoning, *un homme*—
Often the lustrous form
conceals essential weaknesses
known only to the block.
I know mine; I confess,
to give hypocrisy the lie;
and yet
I judge me worthy to be bought,
and worthier still than most
artworks in the galleries of life
to grace your mansion
and regale your soul.

No. 7

One's secret flaws are half the truth.
One's secret vict'ries o'er oneself,

one's secret kindnesses—
the million touches that unseen

enhance the garden of one's life:
this too is truth.

No. 8

We thrive on trivia;
obelisks stand on sand

and atoms make the universe.
    I weave fantastic futures out of flimsy words,
promise myself pleasures,
            travels,

        and accomplishments,
all on the strength of fantasies,
                conditionals;
                of "if"—
if time stand still—
if you love me—

No. 9

- I -

    Lord,
my thanks, profusely.

- II -

    Lord,
I've suffered endlessly,
have only sores to show the seer.
My emptiness has echoed my own voice.
I've scraped my innards to feed all,
and have gone hungry.
I hurt—

- III -

My heart beats faster
sensing what could be,
what I would have be were I god—
be filled, not fully (like the gods),
just more than am.

- IV -

Lord,
my wish be done on earth
as yours in heav'n.
Amen!

No. 10

It's a long way to the Western tip
of Moses,
where the jetty pierces the sea.

It seems it's always a long way
to the end,
to whatever vision is vouchsafed—
a long way to Montauk, in the East,
where we slowly lose the land
that earths us from the sea.
It's always a long way,
and it's always sands
that waste themselves into the sea,
and so deceptive;
were it not
that the lighthouse hastens to the sea,
inch by inch
year after year,
we wouldn't miss the sands that disappear
year after year.
And to the West, again,
after the long way to the Western tip
of Moses,
we always meet the contrast
between the furious ocean to the left
and, to the right,

the tranquil waters of the bay—
between the devil and the deep blue sea.
    The contrast's there, always, at the end,
after the long walk to the tip
where the jetty splits the water
at Moses.

Life's a long way, too,
whether to East or West,
whether to waste or contrast
between the ocean and the bay—
    It must have seemed so, too,
to Ulysses in th' Ionian sea,
brought, after a long way,
between the crunching rocks,
Skylla, Charybdis,
mere names like Montauk, Moses,
for the place we come to, always,
and the fact:
waste or dismemberment—
at any rate, denial;
what we come to, always,
after a long way.

No. 11

    "Blessed the patient, for they shall live
happily ever after"—
(though the Spanish think
tomorrow's the route to never,
and ever after is disguised
in mists of the mind's creation).
    They don't spell out what they did
when they lived happily ever after,
which is how all stories end

or used to end, perhaps, until
we asked just what it was they did
when they lived happily ever after.
    Few live happily, after all.
    Most live unsatisfied,
and so they die;
and so the priests proclaim
that the happy ever after
is, after all, after earth—
    I had dreamed that I could dream
dreams of an ever after
where wishes could be fulfilled
and I would finally live
happily ever after.

No. 12

    You'd expect to see the sun rise
when you climb Tiger Hill,[8]
and every puffy little cloud
lights up in quick succession
from the distant unimpeded East
to overhead,
and past, beyond your back,
to Everest;

and tourists oooh! and aaah!
and cameras click and whir,
and Hindus *Namaste*[9] the sun
'midst the mumbling and the hum
of ancient mantras.

---

8 A peak north-east of Darjeeling, in the Himalayas, 14,500 feet above sea level. [Ed.]

9 "Greetings!" (Lit., "I bow to you"). Words said as Indians join palms and salute each other or, in this case, the rising sun. [Ed.]

But most of the time there's mist
when you climb Tiger Hill,
so you see nothing.

No. 13

I wonder why the sky laments
sometimes, its visage dims;
it wrings its wat'ry muscle
and unabashedly deplores
whate'er it fancies is amiss;
inconsolable,
it can't contain itself,
and sprinkles salty tears,
now and then,
throughout the day.
Though I don't know what ails it,
what dampens its stupendous flair,
what lurks behind the sunny surface
of its usual daily air,
I grieve with it.
Perhaps
it's just a feeling that we share,
some common wonderment,
some extra-ordinary care
that makes us think, nay, sense
that tears spring forth from some unfair
condition of the soul,
some puzzlement,
some something that imbues despair—
that tears sometimes dispel,
or soothe—
like balsam of a kind most rare
upon a wizened wound.

No. 14

- I -

They knew what they were doing
(one can't forgive them, then)
when they condemned Tantalus to thirst
for waters he could never scoop,
and hunger for delicious fruit,
pears, apples, plums, pomegranates,
lifted forever from his grasp
by gentle winds.
They tantalized
the cunning, callous Titan—
thief of Olympian nectars, cruel
concocter of Corinthian stew—
and cruel, themselves, they
tempt him still, and will for ever
punish him exquisitely,

distantly,
without a torture chamber or a rack,
with simple Nature things,
the water's ebb and flow,
the breezes of th' eternal Paradise.

Any lure denied is torture
to a man: a woman's thigh
exposed, a woman's breast
(a faintly figured promontory
'neath a flimsy dress)
torments the lover's hand
that must not guess what eyes
within its scope confess—
such could have been his punishment
had his sin been lust: to reach for her—

not Clytia, not Dione, but *her*
he could not have—for ever, and for ever,
and for aye.

But he could hunger,
thirst, and lust, and scream
his disappointment to the gods,
scream his frustration: *this*,
at least, he had,
a consolation
devoutly to be wish'd.
Thus, in his wretchedness,
he's not the wretch'dest wretch.

O wretched Tantalus,
I envy not your thirst,
your hunger, or your lust,
only the angry roar of your unrest.

- II -

Tristan, the medieval knight
in jousts before the lady of his dreams,
Iseult, his Dulcinea; and he,
another Tantalus reborn
upon such contravening times,
a-burn with cravings and desires
undemonstrable; and she aware
that she's the lure and the impediment,
aflame, in turn, for him,
his presence her perennial love
undemonstrable, their stations such
whether they lust too little or too much.

At least they knew
the curse that rested on them both;

at least the Nurse mistook
the potion; she knew not
(one can forgive her, then)
what she condemned them to:
unalterable passion unfulfilled
and always the pretense of other loves:
another man, for her, and for the squire,
the lovely White Iseult's most sweet desire.

Ah, Tristan, Tantalus of later times,
you could not vent your passion
nor your disappointment, yet you had
the certainty of retribution: she loved back,
she lusted, too, for you, felt tantalized
as much.
I envy not the silence
of your crave, nor, worst of all,
the feigning of another love;
but retribution, just the sense of it,
an intimation, even—
ah,

what sweet revenge 'twould be
for all the wasted, secret, solitary lust.

No. 15

- I -

"Wild wild Unicorn
whom the Virgin caught and tamed"[10]

that was one legend:

10 These words are from a medieval Latin hymn describing Christ as the Unicorn and the Virgin Mary as his mother. See Harding, *Woman's Mysteries*, 51. [Ed.]

he oneness hypostatized,
she the mother virginal,
his tapestried, encircling stall;
the myth tamed, thus, reduced
to common terms.

Asperges me, Domine, et mundabor[11]:
all legends must be laved
in the baptismal font of censorship,
transformed
and rendered harmless by interpretation:
"that's why no horn was found;
the beast's not real, just surreal,"
they said; "Father, Son (you see?),
and Holy Ghost. Amen."

The truth, however, more surreal still:
the Unicorn had not been caught
because he'd never found
the virgin's mesmerizing lap,

lure and perdition,
alone assuring capture.

Ah, but he (the Unicorn) had yearned for her
—her lap—
as sailors yearn for haven. Yet,
what beauty would consider him,
what bosom cradle that enormous head
athwart which stood erect
the monstrous protuberance?
Would a virgin not conceive
fear, at least, reclined
with Priapus in her lap?

---

11 "Sprinkle me, Lord, and I shall be cleaned." *Psalm* 51:7. [Ed.]

One must see this
from the Unicorn's point of view:
he was a beast, unsightly,
yearning to be loved;
the virgin's welcome was a wish,
a hope,
a consummation
devoutly to be wish'd.

- II -

In te domina speravi
non confundar in aeternum[12]
I will not be disappointed
in aeternum
I have trusted in the maiden
non confundar in aeternum
I am certain that thou livest my redeemer
in aeternum
In my flesh I know I'll see thee
non confundar in aeternum
In thy bosom I will lay me
in aeternum
In thy lap I will be cuddled
in aeternum
In te domina speravi
non confundar in aeternum

- III -

There was a man once had a Unicorn. He lived on an island, and there was none other with him on that island save the Unicorn.

12 "In thee, Lady, I have hoped: I will not forever be denied": paraphrase of *Psalm* 31:1. Other references are to *Job* 19:25-27. [Ed.]

The man was gentle and caring. He procured whatever he might for the beast in his keep. Whatever the beast required, the man gave it him, for he was a loving man, and he thought not of himself first, but of the Unicorn.

The Unicorn grew strong and healthy, and his coat was white all over, and it shone like a ray of moonlight on the dark waters of a pond at midnight. Everything in him was white, and he had not soiled his horn, for there were no enemies on the land.

At the height of his nature's powers the Unicorn yearned for a maiden's lap on which to rest his cornute head, for he wished to be tamed. When his strength was greatest and his urges wildest, he sought to be pacified. But there was no maiden to be found on the island; in all the span of the land there was no woman to behold.

So the man became a maiden. Out of his love for the Unicorn he became a maiden, and the Unicorn drew near and rested his horned head on the maiden's lap; on her lap he rested.

And on that day she tamed him.

- IV -

Ulysses loved Penelope,
his absent lap in distant Ithaca—
the preferable[13] heaven,
earthly, fleshly, perishable
he hoped to reach if Neptune dozed;

13 The reference is to Ulysses' refusal of Calypso's offer of immortality because he "preferred" Ithaca (*Odyssey* VI., 257-258). [Ed.]

the bed of ancient olive wood,
sky-canopied, hand-carved,[14]
uncertain terminus of his long search
past Sirens, Nymphs,
and Nausicaä's blush—

his hope, to reach irrévocably
what he irrévocably loved,
however doubtful,
however much it cost
to spurn Calypso, Circe,
laps divinely proffered,
to gain th' uncertain, aging matrix.

And she,
despite his rumored death,
despite the youthful stallions
pawing at her doorstep,
waits for her wild Unicorn
weaving unendingly
the tapestry of *her* hope.

- V -

"Where there is hope there is religion."[15]

Pygmalion hopes: he waits her advent,
celebrates her rising in the spring,
prays for her Pentecost,
adores her mystic body glorified,
believes her incarnation,
death and resurrection,

14 *Odyssey* XXIII., 181. [Ed.]

15 Attributed to Ernst Bloch. [Ed.]

that hope will save him from the damned,[16]
that she will come a second time
(nay, many more!)
to raise him from the dead.[17]

For she has said:
"My faithfulness,
my steadfast love
shall be with him, and in my name
his horn shall be exalted."[18]
Come, Lady, come!
Wilt thou hide thyself for ever?
How long will thy wrath burn like fire?
Remember what the measure of life is,
for what vanity thou didst make
all the children of Eve!
Who can live and not see death?

Who can deliver our souls from the gaols of Sheol?[19]
Life is a long patience.
Come, Lady, come!
Mârina tha![20]

- VI -

Saint Pygmalion: pray for us.
Saint Florentino: pray for us.

16 "We are saved by hope" (Romans 8:19). [Ed.]

17 See García Márquez, *Love in the Time of Cholera*, 340: "She took the final step: she reached for him where he was not, she reached again without hope, and she found him unarmed. 'It's dead,' he said." [Ed.]

18 *Psalm* 89:24. [Ed.]

19 Paraphrase of *Psalm* 89:46-48. [Ed.]

20 See *1 Corinthians* 16:20: "*Mârana tha*!" ("Lord, come!"). "*Mâra*" means "Lord" in Aramaic. *Mâri* is one of the names of the ancient Goddess. [Ed.]

He had remained a virgin (!)[21]
for her; he courted her still,
writing her name
on the petals of camellias,
aboard the *New Fidelity*,
built on the hopes of years
—seventy-six, to be exact—

Saint Fermina: pray for us.

Would they be lovers, then?
Would life prevent their sunder
in aeternum?
Saint Ulysses: pray for us.

Would they keep going, going, going[22]—

Saint Penelope: pray for us.

weaving this time unendingly a tapestry of *their* love?

"A consummation/devoutly to be wish'd." Jones remembered the passage from *Hamlet*. In fact, he recalled that the passage had to do with sleep, with dreams, and with the uncertainty of both death and dreams. The question it raised was whether it was wise to exchange calamitous reality for the unknown realm of death, which was like the exchange of wakeful living for dreams whose essence we could not predict and which might turn out to be anxious

21 Marquez, *Love in the Time of Cholera*, 339. [Ed.]
22 Marquez, *Love in the Time of Cholera*, 324, 348. [Ed.]

or frightful visions. The end of pain was, indeed, "a consummation/devoutly to be wish'd," just as the realization of some dreams, their "consummation" was something one could desire, or even hope for. But there was a risk, too, in leaving reality for the fanciful realm of the imaginary. At any rate, it appeared that the context of the quotation seemed to indicate, as Pickering maintained, that the *Elegies* dealt with fantasy, with a wished-for world beyond that of everyday, humdrum existence. The sexual content of the *Elegies*, therefore, was of "such stuff as dreams are made of." At worst, one might call them sublimations. Freud, after all, had written that only unsatisfied people dream and fantasize. Jones thought this was an over-generalization, but Freud certainly had a point.

How to interpret the sexual aspects of the first five poems? "No. 1" was harmless enough, a poem of friendship in the same vein as the much older sonnets. Even "No. 2" could be interpreted along the same lines. But "No. 3" spoke of a definitely stronger attraction, though making a careful distinction between "lust" and "love," and hinting at the transformation of the former into the latter ("Sin turned to grace") in ways that even Plato might have commended. In fact, as Pickering had noted, Morrison had used a passage from *Republic*. The poem could have been taken, even, as an elaboration of Socrates's quest for the beauteous soul beyond the gorgeous body of Charmides. "No. 4," however, was unabashedly sexual. Still, had it not been for the fact that Morrison had shown it to his actress friend, it could have easily been taken as the artistic expression of marital sexuality. Morrison, after all, *was* married. Finally, "No. 5," sexual though it was, was patently fanciful. The word "virginal" (contradictory in the context) made that clear, and the concluding lines left no room for doubt. So what was all the fuss about the *Elegies*?

Clearly, he thought, the "fuss" was not about the poems themselves. It stemmed from the fact that the object of the fantasies was known, though her name had never been divulged. The fantasies, thus, were *real* fantasies, not the kind most people thought poets wrote—exaggerations of romantic souls, but at bottom sentimental drivel. Morrison was here exposed as a man with fantasies, with wishes unfulfilled, with pain due to frustration at having to live in fantasy what he would have liked to live in reality. The *fuss* was that the *Elegies* revealed Morrison to be like everybody else: yearning to live "happily ever after," knowing—or at least suspecting—that this would never be, that such a "consummation," no matter how devoutly wished, was a thing for which one merely hoped.

That was also the essence of "No. 15," the "hope" poem. Jones didn't necessarily agree with all the interpretations Pickering had concocted; some of them seemed far-fetched. But the main lines of the poem were clear. It expressed a solid hope that wished-for fantasy might come to pass. In this, the poem was but an elaboration of everybody's state of mind. Everybody lived with some degree of dissatisfaction; everybody dreamed of further or higher fulfillment; everybody hoped that someday, somewhere, all wishes would be fulfilled.

Most people expressed their hopes in trivial manners: buying tickets for the lottery, watching soaps on TV, reading cheap Gothic novels, even praying ("keeping your fingers crossed" was a disguised expression of hope); some, on the other hand, expressed their dreams in refined language, in exalted terms, drawing images and metaphors from the classics, identifying with the traditional heroes of expectancy—Odysseus, Pygmalion, Sir Gawain, young Faversham (one of his most favorite characters in all literature), Don Florentino, even Faust, with his inverted hope to live fulfilled but die unsatisfied, and thus avoid eternal unfulfillment. To be like them was, in itself, a dream that most people dreamed but shaped in diverse ways: they hoped to be like the lucky millionaire next door; like the couples on TV, screaming wildly because they had just won the sweepstakes. Such hoping was fine for most people, but not for mystics and saints. The common wisdom seemed to maintain that mystics and saints had no business having fancies, dreams, or expectations beyond those connected with a heavenly eternity. Their lot was to live a life without illusions, or, if that was impossible, a life in which all dreams were holy. Sexual fantasies were unbecoming to the saint; in fact, Christianity had labeled these desires as sin to be dutifully avoided. Still, that Morrison had given expression to them in his poetry was understandable, even if for some it was scandalous. And their presence proved nothing one way or the other about Morrison's sanctity. The "truth" about Morrison could not be settled by this evidence. Further investigation was necessary.

It seemed to Jones that he would get nowhere until he had ascertained what had actually happened between Morrison and the mysterious actress. The biographers had insisted that there had been no sexual involvement. Pickering concurred. Very well. But something else had happened, though he didn't know what, and it was a crucial piece of the puzzle that was Morrison. Without that piece, he could not make a justifiable recommendation to the bishop. He had to investigate the event more fully before reaching a conclusion, and the obvious sources of truth were the biographers, Morrison's widow, and the mysterious actress herself.

Jones turned his attention to them.

CHAPTER FOUR

After a couple of phone calls, Jones arranged to meet with Ann Morrison. She still lived in the Bronx, on the Grand Concourse. Jones took the elevator up to the sixth floor and rang the bell at the apartment door.

Mrs. Morrison opened the door and invited him in. She was now in her late eighties, frail and somewhat stooped, but she retained a quiet dignity. Jones noted that the apartment was spotlessly clean and that all the books were lined neatly on their shelves. The furniture was old but attractive, appearing to be in excellent condition. The brilliant colors of the rugs were immaculately maintained. Every detail conveyed the impression of meticulous care.

After some pleasantries had been exchanged, Jones inquired of Mrs. Morrison if he could ask her a few questions about her husband.

"Of course, of course," she answered genially. "But you know," she added, "nobody has shown interest in Bill for years."

Jones assured her that there had been interest in Morrison's work, even though she had not been contacted. "The details of his life are well known. It's the quality of his work that now occupies scholars and other artists," he added. He couldn't tell her, of course, that there was another cause for interest in Morrison—the matter of his sanctity.

"What kind of man was Bill?" Jones wanted to know.

"Oh, he was wonderful, very easy to live with, very accommodating. Of course, he did have a temper, but it flared up less and less as he grew older. In his mature years, he had become much centered, very spiritual, in a strange sort of way."

"Can you explain that?" inquired Jones.

"Well, he seemed to have attained peace with himself, though he was never at peace with the world. He had learned to accept himself, but he was unwilling to accept the silence and the absurdity of the world. He had always protested injustice, and he came to think of death as the most unjust factor of existence. He believed it was unfair that we should all die indiscriminately, the good as well as the bad, heroes as well as cowards. And even though he agreed that the inevitability of death conferred a degree of equality on the whole human race, he was unwilling to accept equality, and not justice, as the goal of life."

"But he was inwardly at peace?"

"Yes, yes, very much so," she said. "He had achieved a certain detachment which protected him from changes in his environment, even when he railed against them. And he had developed a great, innocent love toward those around him, on whom he poured his affection almost without distinction. Oh, he had his favorites," she added with a smile, "his really close friends, with whom he would joke and be silly, whom he would hug and kiss, and to whom he would unequivocally say, *I love you.*"

There was a brief pause, as if she were relishing the vision of past revelries.

"Did he do anything . . . extraordinary?" Jones asked.

"Miraculous?" she interposed with a reassuring smile.

"Yes!" he said with an almost audible feeling of relief, for he wouldn't have felt comfortable using that word.

"He didn't turn water into wine," she responded after another thoughtful pause, "if that's what you are asking. Some people said he worked miracles with the young, but that's because they only saw the results. They never witnessed the endless conversations . . ."

Her voice trailed off as she looked away.

Again, Jones interrupted her musings. "Was he a mystic?"

"To be a mystic is to be initiated into the mysteries, whether in ritual or through your own experiences . . . Yes, he was a mystic. He passed as easily from one state of consciousness to another as others fall asleep and wake up. And he always seemed ready to see beyond the appearances of things, persons, and events."

"You speak of him as if he had been a saint."

She smiled at that. "It depends what you mean by a *saint*," she replied firmly, with almost a hint of defiance in her voice. "You see, Bill did not put faith in canonizations and declarations. What mattered to him was to *be* a saint.

"More than a saint, he wanted to be a full human being, someone who rose to the heights of ecstasy as well as plumbed the depths of misery, someone who knew how to suffer, someone who . . . created himself out of his own matter, according to the vision of his own imagination. Not an easy thing to do, Mr. Jones, not an easy thing."

"Did he achieve these goals?"

"No, goodness, no," she said, laughing, "but he was closing in on himself, like a hunter on his prey. He had himself covered. You see," she said, mimicking the actions of a hunter taking aim, "he was continually adjusting and refining his aim."

"I see," said Jones.

"You may be interested to know," she continued after a pause, "what he was reading when he died."

"I know he was reading Nietzsche."

"Ah," she said contentedly, "you have read his biography. Would you care to see his study?"

"I would love to," answered Jones. They stood up, and he followed the widow into an adjacent room full of books, neatly stacked, immaculately clean. To the side was an old campaign desk, and on it a book lay open.

"I have tried to keep things as much as possible as they were when Bill died," she said.

Jones looked around in silence at the enormous effort of love over so many years and, eventually, moved towards the desk. Without picking it up, he peered at the open book, noting the pages to which it was open.

"Thank you," he said, "for letting me see this."

They returned to the living room and sat down again. Making it sound as casual as he could, Jones asked, "May I ask about the affair with the actress? What is the truth concerning it?"

"The truth, Mr. Jones," she answered, unperturbed, "is that I knew nothing about it. Moreover, there was no affair. Bill met dozens of people at those talk shows his publisher arranged for him, and he sometimes would mention a name or two to me, nothing more. He may have told me her name, but I do not recall."

"Did you watch the shows?"

"Sometimes I did," she said, pausing as if she were trying to remember. "Unless they came on at three o'clock in the morning," she added with a chuckle. "She could have been in any of a number of shows, you know, with other writers and poets."

"Did you watch any of her movies?" Jones asked, realizing as he did that his question made no sense, since they did not know the name of the actress. He corrected himself, "I mean, did you tie her to any of the movies you both saw?"

"We didn't go to the movies much. It could have been any, you know. As I told you, there was nothing special about any of them, which is why the news of an *affair* was something of a surprise. It was the biographers who discovered the thing and queried Bill about it, but not in my presence. And by the time the books were out, Billy was dead. That's the truth, Mr. Jones."

"Morrison never showed you the *Elegies*?"

"No, Mr. Jones. I read them for the first time when I was going through his papers with Pickering."

"Were you shocked?" he asked, cautiously. "What was your reaction?"

"I took them for what they were—healthy fantasies. You see, he would have been dead without fantasies. The imagination was his life. He used to enjoy quoting Blake, 'The imagination is the human existence itself.'"

How beautiful, Jones thought to himself, *perhaps too beautiful, too wonderful*. But then again, he had not known Morrison.

Here he was trying to capture the essence and the truth of Morrison and being stymied in the process. The widow was happy with herself and with the life she had lived with Morrison.

Twenty-three years of mulling over details after his death had been more than enough to smooth out the sharp edges of Morrison's life, so that only the roundness remained, a roundness that inflicted no pain. He wouldn't get any critical view of Morrison this way. He had to look elsewhere.

Jones refrained from asking any probing or possibly upsetting questions. The widow was entitled to her memories and to the picture of Morrison she had painted from the bits and pieces of his life. It would have been unethical to reach his conclusions at the expense of upsetting hers. Eventually, he thanked her profusely for her cooperation, expressed his pleasure at having met her, said good-bye, and left.

* * *

Back in his own apartment, Jones had tried to devise a plan to contact the biographers for whatever additional information they might possess. A first step would be to contact the publishing houses that had printed the books, to find out if royalty checks were still being mailed to the authors, and, if so, where. Of course, there was a chance that the royalty checks were going to heirs, but that in itself would be an important bit of information.

The company that had published *A Poet's Life* had gone out of business, but its titles had been taken over by another publishing house. The companies that had published the other two biographies had merged with larger ones, so the process of unraveling the threads took several days. It didn't help, either, that all three books were out of print and had not circulated for quite a few years, so that royalty checks had not been issued to anyone for some time. Still, two of the original authors did not appear as recipients of the last checks issued, which would indicate that they had died. To make sure, he wrote letters of inquiry to the last extant addresses, and, after several weeks, received replies stating that both authors had indeed died. The third letter of inquiry remained unanswered for quite a while; in fact, Jones had almost given up on getting any information from this quarter when he received a note indicating that the third author was still alive, but was suffering from Alzheimer's disease and couldn't remember anything about the past. To make sure, he wrote a letter to the nursing home where she was spending her remaining years, inquiring about her condition, only to receive a curt note stating that it was the policy of the home not to give out information on any of their resident patients. Unwittingly, however, they had confirmed the news he had received: that she was confined to the home and was unable to communicate by herself.

* * *

The only remaining source was the actress. It was difficult to doubt her existence, since all three biographers had mentioned her, and all three had refused to disclose her name. No details were provided that might have given him a clue as to her identity and whereabouts. The only usable fact mentioned was that she and Morrison had met at promotional shows and parties connected with his books. He surmised that the shows would also have been geared to promoting her career.

Jones had a strange feeling about embarking on this search for the actress. He hadn't felt any qualms about tracking the biographers, but this was somewhat different. After all, Morrison himself had not named her; in fact, it appeared he had written the *Elegies* with the intention of never showing them to her as long as he lived, though he later changed his mind and showed her drafts of at least some of them, with the disastrous consequences already noted. How had the biographers gotten hold of her name? Had Morrison given it to them, perhaps with the express understanding that they would never divulge it? Why had he done that? Had she herself agreed to speak to them on condition of strict anonymity? So what right had he to uncover what so many had tried so hard to cover?

He also thought of Morrison's feelings, how painful it must have been for him to keep her name secret when he loved her so much. He remembered St. Augustine writing extensively in his

Confessions about the woman with whom he had lived for some twelve or fourteen years, whom he had brought from Carthage to Milan, and with whom he had had a son. Class differences prevented him from marrying her, and he had been forced to send her back to Africa on the pretext of wedding a young girl of exalted social standing.

In the midst of these thoughts, Jones rose from his chair and picked Augustine's *Confessions* from one of the shelves in his study. He walked back to his seat, leafing through the book, looking for the pertinent passage. He found it, toward the end of Book VI, and he read: "The woman I slept with being torn from my side as a hindrance to my marriage, my heart which clave unto her was torn and left wounded and bleeding."

Jones closed the book, closed his eyes, and wondered how even at that painful moment, Augustine could have refused to name her. Surely, others knew her name; after all, they had lived together, he and she. But he had not named her, even though his heart was rent by the separation. So her name was unknown to posterity. And so too would the name of Morrison's "woman" disappear if he did nothing to find her, or if his efforts miscarried. And again the question surfaced: what right did he have to bring to light what others had deliberately obscured?

But, like Augustine, Morrison had at least acknowledged her, her existence, his love, his pain, his hope. He had acknowledged what belonged to him, leaving her secret in her keep. The biographers had understood this and honored his wishes—he must have insisted on it. He, Jones, would do the same. He would search for her, and if he found her, he would also honor Morrison's decision. He would leave her name unpublished. He would concern himself only with what was Morrison's: whether or not he was a saint.

* * *

According to Pickering, the *Elegies* had probably been written in the summer of 1987. If they concerned the actress, as everyone seemed to think, Morrison must have met her one or two years before. Perhaps all Jones had to do was to search for the names of guests at every talk show going back from the summer of 1987.

Somewhat excited now about the prospect of unraveling this mystery, he left his apartment and returned to the public library on 40th Street. After some delays caused by library officials reluctant to produce microfiche records of TV guides going back at least twenty-eight years, he began the laborious process of identifying talk shows and looking for the names of the guests.

He worked his way through records for several days without success. When he came across Morrison's name a couple of times, the other guests were either not women, or did not appear again as guests with him, violating his hypothesis that Morrison and the actress would have had to have appeared more than one time together before anything could develop.

Then, he found the name of a woman appearing twice with Morrison in fairly quick succession; she appeared again, by herself, a couple more times. She even appeared both by herself and with Morrison several times *after* the summer of 1987. The name was Julie Carter.

Excited, almost unable to contain himself, Jones searched the indices of actors and actresses and the movies they had starred in. Julie Carter had appeared in a number of movies, most of them not illustrious, but some quite famous, like *Field of Honor*, *Star Trek XIII*, and *The Aftermath.* She had appeared in movies that would have been widely advertised and distributed. Critical reviews had appeared in many magazines, and Morrison must have read at least some of them. It was tempting to speculate whether or not Morrison had seen her act, and in what role; if he had liked her acting; and whether his impression from the films had played a part in their becoming friends, once they met.

She was very attractive, Jones discovered. Could it be that Morrison was mesmerized by her beauty and the sensuality her body exuded, especially if he had seen her act? Had he watched her undress in *Field of Honor* and draw close to Frank Guevara, who had kissed her passionately before they both succumbed to their passions? That might explain why their friendship had blossomed so rapidly. He might have watched her defenseless in her nakedness, and she might have found him unprotected in the transparency of his poems (if she had read any of them), so that they had penetrated very quickly to the core of their beings and instantly felt safe with each other—one of the basic building blocks of love. This was all speculation, of course, but at least he now had a name. That was the important thing.

With this information in hand, he decided to follow the same procedure he had employed with the biographers: the films in which she had appeared were still being shown, and she must be receiving royalty (or residuals) checks from the producers. All he had to do was find the address to which the last check had been mailed, and he would be on to something.

However, things proved more complicated than he had expected. The checks were being placed directly, by electronic transfer, into a bank account. To get her address from the bank, he would have to first find out where the bank was located. This involved a visit to a national registry of banks kept by the Federal Banking Commission, where he was able to ascertain that the code number placed the bank in Maine, in the small town of Waterville. He wrote the bank asking for her address, knowing full well that the bank would refuse, but hoping they would tell her that there had been an inquiry about her whereabouts, perhaps mention his name to her. At the same time he dispatched a brief letter to her, addressed simply:

Julie Carter
Waterville, ME 04901

To his surprise, the letter was not returned.

Next, he decided to drive up to Maine to initiate a search on the spot. He reserved a room at the local Howard Johnson's on Main Street, rented a car, and, ten hours later, was excitedly paging through the local phone book looking for Miss Carter's phone number and address.

Outside, the weather was frigid. The entire countryside was covered with two or three feet of snow, and the temperature hovered around fifteen degrees. Inside, in his room, he felt cozy and contented, with a certain sense that his search would soon end.

He found an address for a Julie Carter on the outskirts of town, on the way to Thomas College. To his surprise, he also found a phone number. He had thought the number would be unlisted. But perhaps Miss Carter felt sure no one would track her here, so she hadn't taken that additional precaution.

He picked up the receiver and dialed the number. She should be home, he thought, due to the heavy snow and the cold. After a few rings, a woman's voice answered quietly, "Hello?"

"Miss Carter?"

"Yes?" Her tone betrayed surprise, perhaps at not being able to recognize the caller's voice. She probably received very few calls, and only from people whose voices she knew. But here was a stranger's voice.

"Miss Carter," Jones continued, "excuse me, ma'am, but I wonder if I could ask you a couple of questions?"

"Who are you? Are you a reporter?"

"No, Miss Carter, I am not a reporter, have never been a reporter, and do not work for a newspaper. However," he added, "I am after some information and was wondering if I could drop by and chat with you for a while."

"I don't have any information to give. If you need information about me, you can contact my agent."

Drat, thought Jones, *that was one source I neglected to tap. Actresses have agents until they die!* He was exhilarated, however, because, by mentioning her agent, Miss Carter had unwittingly acknowledged that she was an actress.

"Well," said Jones, "the information I need does not concern your acting career."

"What does it concern, Mister . . .?"

"Jones. Jim Jones."

"Mr. Jones," she continued, "I do not trust reporters. I do not give interviews to reporters."

"As I said, I am not a reporter."

"Who are you, then?"

"A good question. I am a writer and teacher," he said, and added quickly, "like your old friend Mr. Morrison."

Miss Carter gasped audibly. She did not say anything for a while, nor did she hang up the phone. Jones was sweating, for his chance at getting the truth from Miss Carter hinged largely on this conversation.

"Miss Carter, I am a friend. I do not wish to disturb you, though, obviously, my call is an intrusion."

"That it is," she had said, with a mixture of resignation and defiance.

"I need to ask you some questions that may help me put in place the pieces of a puzzle."

"What puzzle, Mr. Jones?"

"The puzzle of Morrison, Miss Carter. The puzzle of Morrison."

Again, there was silence at the other end. He endured it for a while, but then he had to speak: "Miss Carter," he said, "this is very important. Would you do me this favor?"

"I don't know you, Mr. Jones, but I suppose—"

"Yes, Miss Carter?"

"I suppose I would lose nothing by meeting you." She paused, and then added with resolve, "Very well. Meet me at my home tomorrow at ten-thirty in the morning."

"Thank you, Miss Carter," Jones mumbled, as he heard the phone click.

CHAPTER FIVE

Jones left the motel at ten, thinking that would allow enough time to drive through town and on the icy roads. The sky was dark, and there was little wind. It felt as if it could begin to snow at any time.

He had asked directions at the desk, and was now approaching a small house in the middle of a large meadow, all covered with snow. He veered from the road and took a dirt path to the house. He parked as close to the house as possible and picked up his briefcase, walked to the entrance, and rung the bell.

"I was expecting you," she said, as she opened the door for him.

She was dressed simply—a long, blue skirt and a white blouse with long sleeves. A dark blue woolen shawl was draped loosely around her shoulders, framing her face and enhancing the color of her eyes. Her hair was short, as it had been in her movies; the gold of it was now broadly mixed with silver, as if by some mysterious alchemy. A solitary diamond adorned each ear. Her eyes, still blue like a piece of morning sky, peered at him inquisitively. Jones could not help noticing how beautiful she still was.

"Well, I did have an appointment," he replied cautiously.

"No, I mean, I was expecting you—someone—to show up at some point to inquire about Bill."

"Why so?" he asked casually as he walked into the living room of the small house. A fire was smoldering in the hearth, and, to the left, a large window ran the length of the room. To the right, the room opened to the kitchen, and a closed door presumably led to a bedroom. There were thick rugs scattered about, and comfortable chairs were placed by the main door and along the window.

"Well," she replied, "I knew I held a key to a part of his life . . . or an aspect of his life, if you prefer. And if Bill's name grew in importance, at some point some intrepid and cunning reporter would be sure to track me down and demand to know."

"I am not a reporter," he said firmly as he took off his snow boots and placed them by the door. He doffed his heavy coat and slung it over a chair, placing his briefcase on top of it.

"Oh, I know," she said, as she motioned for him to sit down. She sat on a chair by the window from which she could easily scan the broad panorama of hills and meadows surrounding her cottage. He felt that was a favorite place of hers, for she settled in it quickly and comfortably. She continued, "You are like the rest of them: like dogs after some juicy morsel of gossip, always after the break that may turn your careers from humdrum to notorious, or even make you famous."

He didn't reply directly to her taunt. She was speaking as if she hadn't heard any of his explanations, as if she hadn't paid attention to anything he had said over the phone. He said again, plainly, slowly, with some deliberation:

"Miss Carter, I am not a reporter."

"Isn't that what they all say," she insisted, "lying, of course, in order to ingratiate themselves with their sources?"

"That may very well be the case," he said, "but I wouldn't really know. I have never interviewed a 'source,' as you call them. And I am after something quite different from gossip or news."

"What are you after, Mr. Jones?"

"The truth."

She tilted her head backwards and laughed, but her laughter rang hollow. It was not sincere. Within it was the nervousness of those who are on guard, always, relentlessly on guard.

"Ah, Mr. Jones," she said presently, "perhaps you still believe in truth. At my age, you see, truth is much too grandiose a word. It's like a tarnished silver trinket whose stains are impossible to clean—you scrub and scrub, and when you think you have eliminated all the dark shadows, a tilt of the piece reveals them right below the luster."

"I didn't say I was after perfection," he replied. "I want to know the truth, what really happened."

"According to whom, Mr. Jones? According to whom?"

"According to you, of course. Morrison is dead, Miss Carter. He has been dead for years. Two of his biographers are dead, and the third has been in a nursing home for some time, suffering from Alzheimer's disease. She doesn't remember a thing. At any rate, they had gleaned the details in their books from you, for the most part, except the parts about Morrison's own feelings. You are their only acknowledged source, and then, as you know, they deliberately left out your name.

He paused briefly, and then continued. "I haven't been able to find any other reference. But you were there. You are the only person who was actually there when it all happened. You are the only one who heard Morrison's confessions. You are the only one who had access to the *Elegies* before their publication. I need the truth of that encounter, Miss Carter. That is the core of my quest."

"And how much are they paying you for it?" she said in an icy voice.

"What do you mean, *they*? Why do you think I would be paid for getting at the truth? I am only paid for what I spend, and I spend very little. Plane tickets, hotels, meals, car rentals—that sort of thing. That's all I get *paid*."

"And *they*?" insisted Miss Carter. "Who are *they*?"

"They are the Chancery clergy, the top clerics of the Diocese."

"Why?" she asked with surprise tinged with suspicion and curiosity, "Why?"

"Morrison had a reputation—"

"I'll say he had one," she quipped.

"No, nothing like that at all," he said. "Morrison had a reputation for holiness, a strange holiness to be sure—the holiness of humanists, perhaps, or of Buddhists—but nonetheless holiness."

"I can't believe that."

"Yes, it's hard to believe. I mean, it must be hard for you to believe it. But he had a faithful following even while still alive. People thought of him as some kind of secular Jesus. Naturally, the publication of the *Elegies* upset many. Questions were raised."

"But the biographies have already spelled out the story about the scandal."

"Yes, indeed, but many have been unsure about the sources. After all, you *disappeared*," Jones said, his gestures placing a pair of invisible quotation marks around the word. "The *Elegies* was another matter altogether. The poems—some of them, at least—left no doubt about the nature of the fantasies. People were upset. Actually, more disappointed than upset. People like their saints flawless."

"But that was more than twenty years ago," she said, turning to face him directly. "Surely, that's not the whole story, the whole reason that you're here."

"No," he answered. He didn't know how much to say at this point, how much to withhold, how much to leave unsaid. "The question is—"

"Yes, yes, what is the question?"

"The question is, should the Church proceed with inquiries into the holiness of Morrison? Was Morrison really a saint? You see, to decide this, one must know what really happened between the two of you."

She straightened up in her chair. An air of distance crept over her whole expression.

"Nothing happened," she said curtly.

"I know that," he retorted quickly. "I am sorry. I didn't mean to cast suspicion on your character or on the nature of your relationship with Morrison. I mean—"

"Nothing happened between Bill and me. Nothing."

There was a certain fierceness in her voice, but also a faint sense of longing, as if she had wanted something to have happened. Her eyes strayed to her right, to the window, and through it to the desolate landscape outside—miles and miles of undulating hills covered with snow, glistening under a dull sky.

"I know, Miss Carter," he said softly, gently. "But you accused Morrison of sexual harassment."

"I did not!" she almost shouted.

Jones fell silent. The sharpness of her rebuke stunned him. Obviously, there were strong and deep feelings dormant in her soul, even after these many years. Once awakened, they could fling themselves at the questioner like mastiffs on a thief. For a long time, neither of them was able to speak.

"I'm sorry," said Miss Carter at last. And she added, "Perhaps we should have a cup of tea. Will you join me?"

"I would be grateful," said Jones.

Miss Carter rose from her chair and moved slowly to the kitchen. She put the kettle on the stove and brought out cups and saucers, which she placed on the kitchen table by the window. From a drawer she produced spoons, and she fetched cream from the refrigerator.

"Shall it be mint or chamomile?" she asked.

"Mint, please," he answered.

"Mint it is," she said genially, as if all tension had been banished from her heart.

The kettle whistled, and she brought it to the table and poured the hot water on the tea bags. The distinct smell of mint floated from the cups.

"You can help yourself to sugar and cream," she said to him. "I prefer mine plain."

He served himself and sat down at the table opposite her, but still with a view of the snowy countryside. For quite a while they just sat there, looking pensively outside, sipping their tea slowly and silently.

"I did not accuse Morrison of sexual harassment," Miss Carter said finally, "though I could have. His actions would have deserved it. But I thought that would have destroyed him, both emotionally and publicly, and that was not my intention at all."

"But surely, Miss Carter, you knew Morrison well enough to realize that sexual harassment would have been the furthest thing from his mind."

"You are wrong," she countered. "You have all been wrong about that. It's part of your male chauvinism to not be able to accept that a man may be guilty despite all his glory. There are no real saints, Mr. Jones. There are no saints."

"Well, that's what I am here to find out. Actually, my goal is much narrower. I just need to know whether or not Morrison was one."

"Would a saint harass a woman?" she asked quietly.

"But that's not what I need to know from you."

"What do you need to know, then?" she asked impatiently.

"Was whatever happened really sexual harassment? That's why I told you earlier that I had come to find the truth, the truth about what happened."

"I just told you, it was sexual harassment. Why won't you accept my word? After all, you have no alternative—you weren't there yourself."

"But the biographers insist Morrison did not mean to harass you."

"What else could his actions mean? He confided in me his sexual fantasies, fantasies which concerned me. The *Elegies* are about me. What else could his actions mean except a subtle form of seduction?" She paused. "*Subtle* is the wrong word. There was nothing subtle about what he said."

"What *did* he say?"

"He said he would like very much to make love to me. Then he corrected himself. He said that what he really would like was to stand before me naked, transparent, with all the innocence and caring of which he was capable, and hold me, shelter me, and make me feel cared for and protected. He had written the same stuff in the *Elegies*." She paused again. "How was I to take that except as an invitation to sex? And given our relationship at the time, what else was that but sexual harassment?"

"But the biographers—"

"The biographers weren't there, Mr. Jones," she interrupted. "They reconstructed what happened from conversations with me and with Bill. I don't think they got much from him before he died."

"Well, they got enough, from whatever source, to cast doubt on your interpretation of events."

She seemed somewhat startled by this, but didn't lose her composure. After a brief pause she said, "No, my perception is accurate. I know what happened."

"But you never spoke to Morrison again, did you? He wrote you a note begging for a chance to explain himself, and you never gave him that chance. Did you feel so sure of your impression that you couldn't entertain the possibility that you had misunderstood him?"

She recoiled, almost imperceptibly. But Jones continued.

"Consider this—you judged the reality of your situation in the context of Morrison's fantasies. The fantasies became your colored glasses. Through them, all his previous actions and all his present actions, appeared tainted to you. His fantasies became reality for you. An innocent kiss became seductive. A friendly touch became a caress. Confidences became invitations. His trust in you became a disarming ploy to get you in bed with him. And how could he deny that he had kissed you on the cheek, or rubbed your shoulders when you were tired? All of this he had done, and more, and it had seemed innocent to you at the time, but now, after his revelation to you of his fantasies, after reading the *Elegies*, you reinterpreted it all anew as sexual harassment. Didn't it occur to you that you were mixing his fantasies with his reality in ways which might never have occurred to him?"

She did not answer him. She sat motionless, looking intently, almost longingly, at the dreary landscape outside the window.

He went on. "Morrison kept his fantasies and his reality separate. That's what the biographers wrote, and they must have known."

"What other evidence is there besides my own?" she repeated.

"Well, for one thing, the very fact that he wrote the *Elegies*. They belonged to the realm of fiction, that is, of fantasy. Originally, he did not mean for you to see them. Later he showed you drafts, and that was because he felt you should know everything about him. They expressed what he wished might be, or might come to be. But he knew well what *was*—the present—and the present between you two was just friendship. Didn't he tell you that? Isn't it conceivable that the reality of his love for you was truly innocent? Isn't it possible that he never really lusted for you, though he wished he could have? He may have hoped to be your lover, but is that proof enough that he was seducing you? If you were to look again at the last kiss he ever gave you without the prejudice awakened in you by the knowledge of his fantasies, could you swear the kiss was sexual?"

She did not answer him. The tea had grown cold now, but it still smelled sweet. Drinking it was a relief, a distraction from the intensity of the moment.

"Why didn't you speak to him again?" he asked.

"Oh, I did speak to him the few times we met on professional assignments, but I snubbed him. I would not even ride in the same car with him, or be in a room alone with him. I made him feel—or I intended to make him feel—that I did not trust him, not anymore."

"Did you really believe that Morrison would have attempted to seduce you, or that he would have attacked you?" he asked. "Surely, you knew him well enough to realize he was incapable of such behavior."

"Yes, I knew him well, perhaps too well. No one ever knew him as I did, and perhaps that's why I recoiled from him. I don't know, it's—"

"Did you know the pain you caused him?"

"I'm not sure I did," she replied, but added quickly, "I just don't know. I should have known, but I was too involved in my own pain."

"Because you thought he was trying to seduce you?"

"Yes, yes. I must have been too involved in my own fantasy to be able to deal with his reality, the reality of what he was, of who he was."

"But you turned against him—in fact, you almost persecuted him," Jones said. "Why?"

"I felt betrayed by him," she acknowledged, sadly.

"Didn't it occur to you that he felt equally betrayed by you? He had trusted you with secrets perhaps only the grave should have known. Or were you perchance afraid to learn the truth?"

"What truth?"

"That he really loved you as his friend, and that his love was the purest you had yet known."

"Maybe . . . I loved him, too, but I was afraid of acknowledging my love for him. I never told him I loved him—*cared* for him, yes—but never *loved*."

"Why?"

"I don't know. I don't know."

Her voice had trailed to a whisper, and her eyes seemed to follow a trail into the distance, through the window, to the snowy hills beyond. He, too, looked outside. It had begun to snow.

"I felt his confessions were an invitation for me to love him beyond the limits I had set for myself," she added slowly, as if she were waking up from a dream. "It really didn't occur to me they could be anything else."

"After all the friendship that had passed between you?"

"Yes, after all that. I was convinced he was wrong. I was sure he wanted to seduce me. I didn't see another explanation . .

. perhaps because I didn't want to see it. In fact, even today, I am unable to say I was wrong. You see," she turned slowly toward him, "I would have to mourn a great loss if I were wrong."

"I see. That's the loss he must have mourned the last years of his life, all in silence, save for the note he wrote to you. Your silence must have felt like condemnation. It must have torn his soul apart."

"I'm sorry," she replied, almost like a whisper.

"I wish he had heard you say that," Jones said, with a sigh.

They remained silent for some time, looking wistfully through the window at the snow falling outside.

"You know," Jones broke the quiet, "before he died he seems to have been re-reading Nietzsche's *Schopenhauer as Educator*." He stood up and looked for his briefcase, which he had left in the living room. He retrieved it and opened it, taking out a small copy of the book. As he walked back to his place, he opened it to a certain page and continued, "His biographers chronicled this, but they neglected to add that at his death, the book was found opened to a particular passage in chapter four. His wife, Ann, showed me. Mind if I read it?"

"Go ahead," she said, as she closed her eyes.

"'A happy life is impossible: the highest obtainable by man is a heroic life. Such a life is led by whoever, in one way or another, fights against very great odds for what is beneficial to all, and ultimately wins, receiving little or no reward. Then at the end he remains petrified . . . but posed nobly and magnanimously. His memory remains, and he is celebrated as a hero; his will, mortified by trouble and work, lack of success and the ingratitude of the world during his lifetime, is extinguished in Nirvana.'"

He closed the book. Her eyes were still closed, but her eyelashes were moist. When she finally opened her eyes again, he said, "He loved you so dearly, and he wanted so much to be your friend."

"I know," she said, "I'm sorry."

All the way down from Maine to New York City, Jones meditated on his conversation with Miss Carter. He hadn't been prepared for what he found—or what he had *not* found. He had expected some kind of elucidation, the solution to the riddle of Morrison's *Elegies*, and he had solved nothing. No answers, no explanations, no new sources or interpretations. Perhaps he had been wrong in hoping that the biographers, or Miss Carter herself, would solve matters for him and give him the response to his query, so that all he had to do was transmit their views to the Bishop, avoiding any real decision on his part. But here he was, pretty much at the end of his inquiry, with no obvious resolution in sight.

It struck him that a major part of the trouble was his own definition of the problem. First, he had made the meetings between Morrison and Miss Carter the centerpiece of his inquiry. He had thought they would provide the definitive clue to the character of Morrison, but they had not. They were an important piece, but not the crucial one he had thought they would be. Second, he had constructed the question of sexual harassment in terms of a confrontation between two ethics: an ethic of objective consequences and an ethic of intention or motive. How was one to judge an action, in terms of the intention of the agent, or in terms of the consequences of the action? If you went through a red light because you *loved* red lights, and in the process killed a person, could your motives excuse the fact of the killing? Obviously not. But when intentions were pure, were you entirely justified in judging an action solely in terms of its objective consequences? Morrison's intentions had been above reproach; that much seemed clear. But the words he had uttered, what he had done, could be deemed objectively questionable. How was the morality of the situation to be adjudicated? Could one conclude that Miss Carter was wrong for not having included Morrison's intentions in her estimate? Could one exculpate Morrison's actions solely by virtue of his innocent intentions?

Jones had tried to be reasonable about the point at issue. Clearly, Morrison's intentions mattered. Equally clearly, the objectivity of his actions mattered. Both had to be taken into account. That was the core of the dilemma. To judge in terms of only one criterion was unfair: it did not give each factor its due. Morrison had, perhaps, been partial to his fancy, while Miss Carter had judged too narrowly according to what she had heard. They were both right, in a sense, and yet both wrong; no one could be right who excluded elements of a case. To exclude was *ipso facto* to be wrong. But what did this elucidation of the problem answer about the case? After all, Morrison had admitted to his sexual fantasies. Ah, but perhaps this was the crux of the matter: were sexual fantasies compatible with a claim to sanctity? Why hadn't he seen this before? He had been asking the question in the wrong way! He had zeroed in on the harassment charge, while the charge presupposed the existence of the fantasies. He had concentrated on the meetings with Miss Carter, while he should have been looking more closely at the writing of the *Elegies*.

Moreover, his approach had been too general. He had asked, was Morrison a saint or a sinner? No one had given him an unequivocal answer. They all had fudged the issue, some by taking refuge in their own views of what sanctity consisted of and some by claiming that the question was ludicrous. And yet there were those—how many he did not know—who kept writing to Bishop Reilly requesting an inquiry into the holiness of the poet.

Morrison's life had been plain and ordinary. But so were the lives of all people. Sometimes we found glamour in the lives of those who stepped in front of the footlights, whether actors or politicians, generals, millionaires, or scientists. However, their lives were still ordinary outside the limelight. They all went to the bathroom and had to eat in order to survive; they all experienced fatigue, hunger, and desires of the body and the mind. In short, they lived like everybody else.

Yet he had to grant that some few people lived their ordinary lives with a heightened degree of intensity. They lived more brilliantly, though it was hard to define their brilliance. Why was Socrates revered more than his friend Alcibiades? What did Plato have that Isocrates had not possessed? What made Joe Namath's play memorable? What made one teacher in a school better than the rest? He couldn't tell. But if he couldn't tell, how could he define sanctity? The things that people normally equated with saintliness—martyrdom, unbounded generosity, profound wisdom—said more about the saint-makers than the sainted. Hadn't St. Augustine said that living well was harder than dying a martyr? Were most of the saints not the product of ages that saw sainthood everywhere—credulous ages that saw only what they wanted to see? Wasn't that the reason for the dearth of saints in modern, objective cultures?

Still, there is a difference between living one's ordinary life without awareness of its ordinariness, and living it with full knowledge of its inadequacy. There is a difference between striving to achieve one's goals and striving with the awareness that all accomplishments are transitory and there is no ultimate perfection. Fancy was the microscope that exposed human achievements as ultimately inadequate, for fancy was able to discover potential in the midst of the most exalted achievements. Only lives lived as if imagined were truly human lives. Blake was right: the imagination was the human existence itself.

The more imaginatively one lived, the closer one came to fulfilling one's potential. Could it be said that the more imaginatively one lived, the closer one came to sanctity? That's what Camus meant, probably, when he asked if one could be a saint without God. That's what Sartre meant by calling Genet a saint. That's why Albert Schweitzer was a saint, but *Saint* Cyril of Alexandria was not (though he had been officially canonized). While Cyril had stifled the potential of Hypatia, whom he had had murdered in the prime of her adulthood, Schweitzer had looked at the totality of his life and discovered potential in a world where most saw only squalor. And he had tied his existence to the creation of a wonderful, unheard of song.

Mrs. Morrison was right. The poet would have shriveled up and died had he not nurtured his soul with the food of images.

Whether the fantasies were sexual or not was unimportant; they were fantasies, and he knew them as such. They made patent his awareness of the incompleteness of his life. Miss Carter had misunderstood them, though she was probably now, even now, coming to realize their importance. And the bishop, perhaps, had been coming to the same realization when he had wondered if *he* was a saint. Being a saint was his fancy, just as loving Miss Carter had been Morrison's, and being outraged was Miss Carter's. Without fancy there was no striving. The point was to dream, for in the dream alone could human existence be fulfilled.

* * *

After his return from Maine, Jones let several days pass, discussing with himself different aspects of this thoughts. He needed time to clarify his thinking and to find a way to convey his conclusion to the Bishop.

Consolidating his insight, Jones came to see the thrust of it more clearly. He found he could even place Morrison's fantasies in the context of other, more exalted, infinitely more polished, but still equally structured, fancies. Dante had been one of the dreamers. He had fallen in love with Beatrice at nine, a love that had remained untarnished and had only been consummated in the extraordinary context of *La Commedia*. The love that had shaken his body to the point of swooning at the tender age of nine had been fulfilled only in the vision of the heavenly Beatrice who had "imparadised" his soul. And Goethe, the philanderer, whose many youthful passions had given rise to the veneries of Faust, had come to fantasize the redemption of his lust and to conclude, equally, that mystical love was the spring that made our human worlds tick and turn. Where Dante had seen the sun and all the stars powered in their orbits by love, Goethe had envisioned the Eternal Feminine, drawing us beyond ourselves in quest of eternal fulfillment.

What difference did it make if the fantasies were sexual? What did the subject matter? Faust had wished to make love to Helen of Troy, whereas Sinclair had fantasized about a young girl whose name he didn't even know, and Morrison had idolized Miss Carter. The point was the power of their fictions, the alchemy of their imaginations. Don Quixote knew the coarse reality of Dulcinea del Toboso, even though his fancy turned her into the lady of his dreams, "*la señora de sus pensamientos*" — the very words Dante had used for Beatrice, "*la gloriosa donna della mia mente*" — Dante, who still fantasized about Beatrice twenty-seven years after having married Gemma Donati! Wasn't that the case, too, with Goldmund, Hesse's sensualist in search of his Madonna, the sum of all his loves and infatuations? And what else was the quest for the Holy Grail? Wasn't sublimation what the troubadours had preached, itinerant priests of love and the imagination, by singing of unrequited desire; that is, of love perpetually unsatisfied but perpetually yearning for fanciful fulfillment? Jesus himself had declared that in heaven marriage would not exist; love, in other words, would be freely given and received. Hadn't he thereby extended an invitation for the imagination to conjure up worlds of sublimated yearning and satisfaction? Wasn't that sufficient grounds to wish devoutly for consummations only fancy could substantialize?

The more Jones thought about all this, the more he became convinced that fancy was the key to Morrison's sanctity. The subject matter of the *Elegies* was secondary; in fact, it was unimportant. If he could see Morrison's fantasies as the expression of his lifelong quest to achieve a radical openness to the ultimate mysteries of existence—what many called the Divine—then he would have to conclude that Morrison was, indeed, on the path to sainthood. The rest was simply a matter of language, of finding the words to state the obvious. That should not be too difficult.

* * *

Finally, after a couple of weeks, conviction set in. Jones, then, typed a brief note to Bishop Reilly. It said, curtly, "He *was* a saint."

CHAPTER SIX

This time the e-mail message had said, "Jim, this is John Reilly. Meet me Tuesday at the Long Island Marriott for lunch, around noon." Jones had called to confirm the date, and his friend had explained that he wanted to discuss Morrison. No secrecy this time, nothing like the conspiratorial circumstances ten years ago.

Jones had arrived early, as was his wont, and he sat down in the lobby to wait for the archbishop —his friend was now head of the diocese.

Presently, his grace appeared, and the two friends greeted each other with their usual glee, joking and patting each other on the back. After a few pleasantries, they walked over to the restaurant and ordered lunch. But it was not until dessert and coffee had been served that the archbishop broached the subject of Morrison.

"I was wondering," he asked Jones, "if you have kept up with Morrison's friend."

"You mean his actress friend?"

"Yes," said the archbishop, "the one who lives in Maine."

"The name is Carter," said Jones, as he dropped a couple of sugar cubes in his coffee, "Julie Carter. I haven't heard from her since the day I interviewed her ten years ago. I haven't written to her, either, so it's not just her fault that we haven't kept in touch."

"You really didn't have to, did you?" commented the archbishop. "You got the information you were after, and that was that."

"That's right." He motioned to his friend to pass the cream, and he poured a little in his coffee. "Why do you ask?"

"Well, I think the time has come to do something more definite about Morrison," the archbishop replied between bites of apple pie.

"Like what?" Jones asked with a twinkle in his eye. "Convene a conference about his work?"

"Oh, stop kidding," said the prelate. "I mean something like holding preliminary inquiries into his sanctity. The requests to initiate proceedings have increased over the past two years."

"Oh, boy," said Jones, "am I glad I am not in your position."

"Why? Didn't you commend him?"

"Of course I did, but that's quite different from canonizing him." He shook his head. "Good grief, John! How long shall we tolerate such antiquated rites?"

"They'll probably go on even after you and I are gone, my friend," the archbishop said with a touch of resignation in his voice. "I've told you, people need such assurances, and I am damned if I'm going to be the one to tell them it doesn't make a bit of difference."

"Aha!" exclaimed Jones mischievously, "do I detect hypocrisy here?"

"Quiet," the Archbishop retorted, smiling, "none of your anti-clerical rhetoric." He finished his apple pie, wiped his mouth, and looked at Jones quizzically. "Do you think you could get a written statement from the woman?"

"What for?"

"Well," he answered, "for the record. I know her views only secondhand, you understand, and that wouldn't be good enough at all. The devil's advocate would call it hearsay, and I could be faulted for not having procured more substantial evidence."

Jones pondered the archbishop's words for a while. When he spoke, his voice expressed concern.

"John, do you really think we should bother her again? The woman must be in her seventies now—if she's even alive. And she may not want to speak to me at all . . . I say *me* because I presume you are going to ask me to contact her, aren't you?"

"My," said the archbishop jovially, "how did you read my mind? That's the very thing I was going to ask you to do."

Jones did not say anything right away. He stirred his coffee slowly, deliberately, looking pensively at the cup. It wasn't simply the thought of disturbing Miss Carter that made him apprehensive, but the very idea of collaborating in an enterprise that he found distasteful and that, for him, symbolized the very decadence of the Church. The ozone layer was decaying; the world's population was over seven billion; thousands of dedicated people were spending their lives ministering to the homeless, the poor, the orphaned and the sick; and all the Church could think of was to waste time on canonization proceedings.

"I know what you are thinking," said his grace, interrupting his friend's musings. "We're fiddling while Rome burns."

"Worse than that. You are pillaging the houses while the city burns. You see, when people are canonized, *we* do not need to keep alive in our minds the memory of their deeds. The official record excuses us, gives us leave to forget. Canonization steals our memories when we need them most. It depersonalizes the holiness of people's lives. That's the last thing anyone should want to do to Morrison—or to anyone, for that matter."

"I understand," said the prelate, "but look, I am only starting the process. I have told you I don't think it will go very far."

"I know," said Jones. "I also know this is your compromise, your bow to tradition, the price you must pay for unhindered action in other matters. It just rubs me the wrong away. That's all."

"Look, you don't have to do a thing. I was just asking. I thought it was advisable to have something in writing from her."

"I know," said Jones again. "I am making a big to-do about nothing. After all, she may even be dead."

The archbishop looked sheepishly at him. "So, you will try to contact her?"

"I guess so," Jones replied, adding pretentiously, with a fawn, "When have I ever denied your wish, your grace?"

The archbishop grinned. He had finished his coffee and pushed the cup and saucer away. "The same financial arrangements apply. And Jim," he added, looking at Jones and reaching across the table to hold his left wrist, "you are still my best friend, you know."

"Some friend," Jones countered, with a smile.

CHAPTER SEVEN

The next day, Jones telephoned Miss Carter. He heard a couple of clicks, then a recorded message came on informing him of a new number that he needed to call. Jones dialed the new number and let the phone ring for a while, but no one picked up. He dialed a second time with the same result, so he decided to try again later. *A minor inconvenience*, he thought of the delay. Surely, Miss Carter was still alive. Whether or not she would be willing to comply with his request was an entirely different matter.

He called again in the late afternoon. After a few rings, Miss Carter's voice answered quietly, "Hello?"

Jones asked, "Miss Carter?"

"Yes?" Her tone betrayed the same surprise laced with suspicion, but this time Jones felt on surer ground.

"Miss Carter, excuse me, ma'am, but I wonder if you remember me. We met ten years ago. My name is Jones, Jim Jones."

There was a short pause. Then, somewhat excitedly, Miss Carter answered, "Yes! Yes! I *do* remember you. How could I forget, Mr. Jones? How could I forget?"

Jones noticed a new quality in her voice, unmistakable though difficult to describe; a barely discernible slowness and a heavier lisping.

"I hope I am not interrupting anything," he said, "and I am sorry for infringing on your privacy."

"Not at all, Mr. Jones. You need not apologize."

"It's been a long time, and I haven't written to you all these years." He paused. "It makes me feel ashamed, calling you out of the blue to ask a favor when you had been so gracious to me ten years ago."

"It's been ten years, has it?" She sighed, ignoring the rest. "My, how time passes."

Jones felt encouraged by the warm reception and the fact that she remembered him. Her pleasure seemed genuine. He felt none of the guardedness that he had sensed the first time they had spoken on the phone.

"Miss Carter . . ."

"Yes?"

"I would like to drive up to Waterville to visit you."

"Goodness, that's a long ride, Mr. Jones. Why would you go to so much trouble?"

He decided to go straight to the point: "It's about Morrison."

"Oh," she said, but he couldn't detect alarm or anguish in her voice, or apprehension. He was prepared for a question about Morrison, but none came. "When would you like to come up?"

"Well," Jones replied, "I could drive up tomorrow, Thursday. I could go by your house on Friday."

"Not too early," she said with a chuckle. "We old folks . . ."

"Don't you worry," said Jones. "I'm not a spring chicken, either. What about late morning? Elevenish?"

"That sounds right."

"Very well," said Jones. "I'll see you Friday."

"I'm looking forward to it," she volunteered, before saying goodbye.

And that was it. He phoned the Howard Johnson's on Main Street, the same one he had stayed at the previous time, and made a reservation. He then remained alone with his thoughts.

He still felt qualms about the whole affair, and Miss Carter's willingness to see him was not exactly what he had expected. Given the tone of their last conversation, it would have been natural for her to avoid him. And yet, she hadn't only consented to see him, she had even appeared happy at the prospect.

But perhaps his apprehension was unfounded. What should he expect but a repeat performance, a mere confirmation of what she had told him ten years ago? At that time her feelings had seemed strong, rooted, not the kind to change; in fact, he had not been able to shake her views of Morrison, though he had tried.

And his own views had been arrived at carefully, logically, and after protracted reflection. So why worry at all? What he needed was, essentially, a transcript of her views, signed and notarized. That shouldn't be difficult at all. What he should do now was pack a few things for the trip and get a good night's sleep, for the drive to Maine would be long and tedious.

And that's exactly what he did, though he couldn't completely shake off a certain feeling of foreboding.

CHAPTER EIGHT

The drive up to Maine was indeed long, but not tedious. It was late summer, and, as he drove farther north, the luscious vegetation bordering the highway began to change, giving but the barest hint of the coming fall. Spaced here and there on the dividing stretch of land between highways were patches of multicolored flowers fluttering gently in the breezes raised by the speeding automobiles. He felt as if he were driving through the countryside of some enchanted region, his eyes regaled by the splashes of color contrasting with the soft green of the meadows and the darker shades of the tall trees. By the time he got on the Maine Turnpike, dusk was beginning to fall, and soon it was dark. He reached Waterville and his motel around nine, had dinner, read, and went early to bed.

He slept late, but got up in plenty of time to complete his morning ablutions, have breakfast, and drive to Miss Carter's by eleven.

In the light of summer, both the town and countryside looked different from the snowy and dreary landscape he remembered. The sun shone brightly, the sky was blue and cloudless, and the temperature was pleasant—even this late in the morning there was a hint of chill in the air. A few new houses had been built on the road to Thomas College, but the main landmarks were still there.

He reached Miss Carter's house, parked on the driveway, and walked to the front door, which was open. He knocked softly and was invited in by a cheery, "Come in, Mr. Jones!"

The living room was exactly as he remembered it, but the long window to the left looked out now on meadows covered with tall, soft grasses undulating gently in the sun.

Miss Carter was as beautiful as ever, though he noticed a few more wrinkles on her face. Her clear, blue eyes had lost nothing of their sheen, but they were set now against a background of almost completely white hair. A solitary diamond adorned each ear, and she wore a multi-colored bracelet on her right wrist. Her outfit, a short-sleeved white blouse and dark blue corduroy pants, belied her true age. She moved gracefully across the room as she came to greet him.

"How nice to see you again, Mr. Jones!"

"The pleasure is mine, Miss Carter," he answered. "It's so kind of you to see me, and at such short notice."

"Well, it's not as if I'm terribly busy up here." She laughed, and Jones sensed that this time nothing was being held back. Her laughter was genuine and joyful, and it made him feel very much at ease. “Do sit down,” she said, as she motioned him towards the chairs by the window. “May I offer you something to drink?”

“No, thank you,” he replied, as he stood looking out the window at the beautiful and peaceful landscape outside. Then, turning to her, he said, “I thought we might talk for a while and then eat lunch.” And he added, “I would be honored if you allowed me to take you out.”

“We could eat lunch here,” she said with a touch of indecisiveness in her voice, which she overcame quickly, adding, “but I would be happy to go out with you.” Then, with a tone of mischief, “It’s not every day I have the pleasure of such charming company.”

Jones smiled. Miss Carter sat down in her usual chair to the right. Jones noticed again the ease with which she settled down. He sat opposite her, with a clear view of the meadows outside. Miss Carter was the first to speak.

“The last time we talked, you were trying to decide if Bill had been a saint,” she said. “What did you conclude? Was he a saint?”

“Yes,” he answered, “that was my conclusion. His fantasies showed him open to the transcendent, to love, to God. This, I decided, was the quintessence of holiness. Since Morrison lived his life immersed in that openness, I had no alternative but to conclude he was a saint.”

She seemed a bit bewildered by his words; whether because his conclusion confused her or because of what it said about Morrison, he couldn't tell. To clear up her doubts, he set out to explain to her the logic of his thinking, the train of thought that had led him to conclude that Morrison had been on the way to sanctity. He told her what he had written to the archbishop, and how he had thought the matter settled until his friend's call the previous week. He shared with her his own apprehensions about the whole business of canonization, and how he disliked the idea of claiming certainty about a person's fate in the afterlife. Finally, he told her the purpose of his visit, how his friend the archbishop had decided to initiate the proceedings, and how he had agreed to request an affidavit from her.

She had listened intently, asking only a few questions here and there to ascertain his meaning, but without making any real comment. He spent a long time recounting his ruminations, and, as his story developed, her expression changed, as if she felt reassured by what she heard.

"Thank you for sharing all this with me. It all makes sense, although I'm not sure I agree with your conclusions or with this canonization business." She paused. "Somehow I still have doubts about sanctity—"

"I do too," Jones interjected, "believe me."

"Let's discuss them later," she said, looking at her watch. "Why don't we go out to lunch now? I'm getting hungry. What about you?"

"Wonderful idea," he rejoined. "I'll drive. You be the guide."

They drove back toward town and crossed the bridge over the Kennebec River. Less than a mile from it, on the eastern shore, was a little restaurant she knew well whose specialty was Maine lobster. They parked in the half-empty lot, went in, and were seated at a table with a breathtaking view of the river sprawling wide into the distance, shining like a broad, silvery ribbon under the warm rays of the afternoon sun.

They settled down, placed their orders, and relaxed while exchanging the usual pleasantries about the locale and the view. Then they grew silent for a while, mesmerized by the scenery and the peaceful atmosphere. Miss Carter was the first to break the silence.

"You know, Mr. Jones," she said to him wistfully, "this may come to you as a surprise, but I have often sat here alone eating lunch, ravished by the beauty of the landscape, wishing Bill were still alive and sitting here with me."

Jones was, indeed, surprised, but he didn't know what to say. He wanted to learn more, but he didn't know what to ask. Sensing his indecision, Miss Carter added, "Ten years is a long time, Mr. Jones. And if one lives alone, one does a lot of thinking."

"I can imagine," he said, wondering if she knew that he too lived alone, "but you seem to have undergone a very definite transformation, a one-hundred-eighty degree turn."

"Perhaps," she replied, and she was going to add something when the waitress came with their red, steaming lobsters and distracted them with the usual banter.

They ate their fill, mostly in silence, speaking only about the food and the landscape. When the meal was finished, they sat languidly at the table, waiting for the check. "You know," said Miss Carter, "as I had started to tell you, living alone, with mostly the elements as companions, forces one to be utterly honest with oneself."

Her voice had a detached quality to it, as if she were speaking to no one in particular. "The river does not answer back," she continued, "nor does the wind or the snow. So, if you want to converse, you must provide answers to your own questions." She paused while she breathed a heavy sigh, whether of regret or resignation Jones could not tell. "No one can best you when you argue with yourself," she added, "for you are the source of your questions and your answers, and the topic of discussion is you."

Jones looked at her for a minute, but decided not to say anything. He didn't feel the need to prod further or to spur her on, for they were in no hurry, and he felt she would say what she wanted in her own sweet time. At last she resumed her soliloquy.

"We are the only witnesses to our inmost thoughts and feelings, Mr. Jones." She became a little more animated as she shifted in her chair and continued, "I have often pitied myself because no one will ever know the small battles I have won over myself, the aches I've had to endure all alone." She looked intently at Jones. "You know, they don't canonize those who bleed every day with no other witnesses to their martyrdom than themselves."

Jones was going to answer when the waitress appeared with the check, which he paid with his credit card from the Diocese, making sure he left a generous tip. He put the card in his wallet while he fumbled silently for the appropriate words.

"Relax," Miss Carter said, noticing his discomfort. "I am at peace with my own obscurity. I have known the limelight and I can assure you it is not more comforting."

"I understand," Jones replied, though in fact he was not sure he did.

"One of the things I've had to confess to myself is that I felt jealousy when Bill was not with me, that in my heart of hearts I wanted him all to myself." She stopped, pondering something. "I take that back. I didn't want him all to myself—I'm not *that* selfish—but I wanted the reassurance that I was *his* friend. I really wanted his friendship, though I was completely unable to admit this even to myself . . ."

"And you went to great lengths to make me think otherwise," Jones said tendentiously.

"Yes, indeed," she replied more animatedly, "because at the time of your last visit I could not admit this to myself."

"But the harassment charge?"

"Which I *didn't* make," she interrupted quickly. "*That* was not faked," she added, resuming her composure. "The feelings I am talking about were completely hidden from myself. In fact, I have come to believe that my outraged reaction to Bill's confessions was a way to mask my own desires and bury them beneath a mound of," she hesitated, but finally blurted, almost apologetically, shaking her head, "of self-righteousness. Ah, Mr. Jones, what ten years of self-scrutiny can do to your pride!"

Jones said nothing. He was awed by the ruthless honesty with which Miss Carter seemed to have analyzed her feelings and was confessing them to him. In fact, he felt humbled by the experience, as if he were witnessing a display of heroic virtue, a kind of martyrdom. For an instant, he entertained the thought that it was Miss Carter who should be canonized, for only a saint could have endured such examination. But he dismissed the idea. After all, millions of people lived such lives of quiet heroism, silent witnesses to their jealousies, longings, hopes, desperations, fruitless loves, and, yes, the primal wish to be confirmed, to have their lives validated by another's love. He wanted to say something to indicate to Miss Carter his appreciation of her, his *fellow feelings*, but he couldn't find the words. He just sat there, looking at the river, twirling a teaspoon, over and over.

While they sat there in silence, satisfied after their meal, lost in the vagaries of their own thoughts, an air of camaraderie had engulfed them. An indefinable sense of oneness and friendliness had penetrated and pervaded them thoroughly. It was so strong it was almost visible in the radiance of their countenances.

They remained in the restaurant for a few minutes more, before leaving in silence, bathed in the glow of the sunny afternoon, basking in the warmth of an inner peace and a profound contentment. They drove back to the house, parked the car, and, still in silence, walked around the front to the edge of the meadow, where the grasses grew tall and their undulating movement made one feel at the very edge of an ocean.

Then they walked back to the house, and, without losing the sense of peace and contentment engendered by the moment, they sat down again by the window, gazing at the rolling hills.

Finally, with an effort, Jones spoke up, "Earlier you seemed to have some qualms about my conclusion that Morrison was a saint. . . . Or perhaps it was about how I came to view sanctity. . . . Is there any other reasonable way to define sanctity?"

"I suppose you're right," she answered, as if waking from a reverie, "though I don't feel closer to a definition of sanctity now than I was ten years ago. If anything, I am even more skeptical about the whole issue of sanctity, especially with regards to Bill. The question seems irrelevant, somehow, or trivial."

"What question would you have asked instead?"

"Whether or not he was my friend—my *best* friend. Your question about Bill's sanctity sidetracked me at first, though I must admit my own meditations about our relationship had been misguided from the start."

"How so?" Jones was beginning to understand how profoundly she had changed, and he was somewhat befuddled by her words. Was this the same woman who had adamantly insisted her perceptions of Morrison were correct? Irrefutably correct? What had brought about this change of opinion?

"I *had* confused his fantasy with his reality, as you pointed out," Miss Carter replied. "It was only after you left, and over a period of years, that I was able to reconsider." She paused briefly. "I have come to very different conclusions."

"Indeed? Even with regard to the charge of sexual harassment?"

"Which I *didn't* make," she insisted again, brusquely, then stopped. "Yes, even about that. You see, I had never really thought about the implications of friendship."

"What do you mean?"

"I have come to see that friendship is larger than mere affection," she explained. "Beyond its private significance, friendship has public consequences. At least, it can."

"You mean—?"

"We are not invisible, Mr. Jones."

"Do you suggest . . ." Jones paused, trying to figure things out. "I am thinking—classical examples come easiest to me—I am thinking of the friendship between Achilles and Patroclus and the effect it had on the Trojan war, or of that between Alcibiades and Socrates, and how Alcibiades's debauchery and treason tainted the public life of Socrates."

"Something like that," she said. "But I mean also that there is risk in loving because loving is public, too."

"Of course."

"Especially between a man and a woman. You see, we women have been warned so often about being on our guard against harassment by men, that even honest men must feel inhibited in expressing their love to their women friends. To do so is to risk a charge—"

"Of sexual harassment," he finished for her.

"Precisely."

Jones was beginning to understand what she meant by the risks of friendship.

"Don't get me wrong," she continued. "Cases of sexual harassment exist. But they are the extremes, Mr. Jones, perversions, no matter how common and pervasive. Charges of sexual harassment and sexual abuse reveal the dangers of engaging the passions and desires, but, at the same time, they obscure the blessings found in relationships that steer clear of extremes."

She paused again, pondering, looking intently through the window as if following a script carved upon the moving grasses. Jones was fascinated, almost bewitched.

"Friendship is a call," she elaborated, "to become one's self in company with another. Bill's confidences, his poems, his honesty about his whimsy for love-making awakened my fear of sexual harassment, and these fears prevented me from seeing what he was offering me: a pure love unashamed of passion and desire, a call to frolic together over the rough terrain still left for us to travel."

"This is some revelation," Jones said, unable to withhold comment any longer. "This is quite a change from your feelings ten years ago."

"Yes," she conceded. "Your questions, which were almost accusations, have helped me see the entire episode in a new light."

He didn't feel his conversation with Miss Carter had come close to an indictment. Still, he *had* queried her insistently, and he had interpreted Morrison's behavior in a manner obviously at odds with hers.

"Why do you deem the issue of sanctity to be irrelevant?" he then asked, trying to gauge even further the extent of her new perceptions.

"I do not deny the nature of fantasy, that it is an openness, but I believe that what was most significant in Bill's case was his longing. He wanted the future. He hoped for it. I have come to understand why love longs for eternity, Mr. Jones—it always wants more. It wants to renew itself forever, and it needs friendship to accomplish this."

Jones felt somewhat confused. Now it was his own interpretation that was being questioned. Quietly, and perhaps even unintentionally, Miss Carter was challenging the conclusions he had arrived at ten years before. He was being forced to swallow a dose of his own medicine.

He reviewed his own conclusions about Morrison. He had come to see the *Elegies* as a work of the imagination—the imagination which, for Morrison, as much as for Blake, was life itself. In this view, he had judged the content irrelevant, for what mattered most was to be open to the future, to possibility—that is, to the divine. But here was Miss Carter saying that the content *was* significant because the content was love, and it is the nature of love to want eternity.

"There is more," Miss Carter was going on. "I have come to see the *Elegies* in a new light."

"What sort of light?"

"I am sure Bill would have liked to make love to me, but I agree with you, Mr. Jones, that at the time, and given the circumstances, the *Elegies* were merely a fantasy, and making love was merely something to be hoped for. But I have also come to see the sexual desires expressed in the *Elegies* as symbolic of Bill's wish to be my friend. That's one thing I failed to see before. Perhaps the crucial thing."

"But it was the sexual aspect of his desire that repelled you!" exclaimed Jones in disbelief.

"I thought so, too," said Miss Carter, "but I have had more time to analyze my feelings. We women, especially, complain about being turned into sex objects and lusted after, but not loved. But on the other hand, who wants to be loved with a purely spiritual love, an abstract and disembodied love that ignores the tingling of the flesh? This was part of my error, too—to be repulsed by passion while longing to be loved. And worse, perhaps, not to have realized that I wanted both: love *and* desire."

"Is that why you never told Morrison you loved him?" asked Jones. "*Cared* for him, yes, but not *loved*?"

"Perhaps," she answered, turning her eyes toward him.

"What guided this re-evaluation of your feelings about Morrison?" asked Jones.

"I told you," she answered, pointing to the outside with a tilt of her head, "this rugged environment in which I live. Also, your relentless examination was a major factor. It thrust open a door through which I could not but walk, regardless of what lay beyond it. Thank goodness, what I found was wholesome."

After a little while, she added, "There is something else."

She got up and moved toward the closed door that Jones had surmised led to her bedroom. She went in, and, from a table by the bedside, she picked up a book. Jones recognized it as the collected poetry of Morrison. Leafing through it, Miss Carter walked back into the living room and resumed her seat by the window.

"Let me read something to you. It was written after the *Elegies*. And, in a way, it is an explication of them. Perhaps one that only I could understand. It is one of the *poems in prose* Bill was fond of writing."

She read:

"I need your young love to stir to flame the smoldering embers of my love!

I need your young body to give my old body strength, to teach it to be supple once again, to run and drink in lustily the fresh and sunny air.

I need your young hand to clasp mine and tell me I am not gone beyond recall. I need your youth to make me young again.

I need your young bosom to rest my tiredness.

I need your arms around me to warm me, for there is a coldness that often creeps upon me as if Death were reaching out to me with icy grasp. I need your fire to fend off that ice.

It was so that Abishag was brought to King David when he was old, and though covered with clothes could not keep warm. And the King knew her not.

I am no king.

Please, be my Abishag!"

She closed the book and looked at Jones, briefly, before turning her eyes toward the west, where the sun was setting slowly.

"You see, Mr. Jones," she said, without turning her head, "everything is there, and it is *so* clear!" She sighed, a mixture of longing and resignation. "He wanted to *feel* loved, and feeling loved meant being *told* he was, yes, but also being made to *feel* it. Yes, he wanted to be hugged. All that talk of sex, fanciful though it may have been—and I agree with you it was a fantasy—was a way of begging for closeness and companionship." She had raised her voice a little, as she picked up the tempo. "If we had lain naked together in bed and hugged each other closely, there would have been no lust in his body or in his soul. I am sure of this now, but," she shook her head softly as if to stress the pity of it all and, more quietly, continued, "this is what the poem taught me. I knew it all before, of course, but somehow I couldn't or wouldn't deal with it."

She had put the book down on the table with a gesture of barely discernible frustration, perhaps at the realization of what could have been. Jones was awed by the subtlety she displayed in the analysis of her feelings and by the details she seemed to have uncovered, as if she were an archaeologist brushing the dirt off a beautiful filigreed statue she had found buried in the sand.

"He loved me, Mr. Jones. He was convinced he was the only man who could have loved me with a pure and generous love, the only man who could have made me truly happy. He said this in so many words in the *Elegies*, but I just would not believe him. Did you notice," she asked, looking down, "that the early sexual poems in the *Elegies* are concerned only with *giving* pleasure to the loved one?" Tilting her head backwards, in a soft voice, she added, "What he wanted most was to make me happy, but for that he needed to be my friend. Friendship was the threshold to everything he deemed wonderful in life, and he wanted for me the best that life and love had to offer.

"There was more, of course. Bill also wanted very much to be my friend, to be reassured that I loved him, that he was *my* friend. Only I couldn't bring myself to tell him. I don't know why. Perhaps it was because I knew *he* wanted me . . . to love him, to tell him. You know," she said, addressing Jones directly, "when we sense people expect us to do something, we feel reluctant, imposed upon. We take their expectations as an intrusion into our space, our emotional space. It's not that we disagree, but that we want to do it because *we* want to do it and not because we are asked. And so we refuse. Then time passes, and, before we know it, life is over, and the opportunity is gone."

Jones wanted to interrupt to console her, to lighten her burden a little, perhaps, to soothe her pain, but she wasn't giving him a chance.

"You know, Mr. Jones, he had written about this in one of his poems, perhaps his best poem, *Narrowness*." She picked up the book again and leafed through its pages, until she found what she wanted. "Here," she said, "listen."

> ". . . . . a quiet, longing query:
> 'Why, why must one be dead, or close to death, to move
> those whom one loves to love? O sickness unto death,
> will never speak of love to living, heed words of life;
> will corpses woo and statues praise; pour forth in absence
> pure sweet delight and reminisce companionship
> in presence never recognized! Some die for love denied;
> more wither for want of kindly words bestowed!'"

"Why didn't I see this? Why?" she asked Jones. "He took a great risk in expressing his love to me, and I just wouldn't acknowledge him. In fact, I turned against him."

She stopped, put the book down, and closed her eyes. Jones couldn't tell whether or not she was crying. After a while, when she resumed talking, Jones felt that her voice sounded the slightest bit shaky.

"The only thing left for me to do now," she said, "is to take hold of my feelings, twined as they are with memories and regrets of long ago. I have examined them very carefully, Mr. Jones, for I don't want to make another mistake." She rose from her seat and placed on the table a small tape recorder which she had picked up from the windowsill.

"Your visit and the request of your friend, the archbishop, have provided me a most welcome opportunity," she said as she turned on the machine. Then, facing Jones, she began deliberately.

"I loved, Bill, Mr. Jones. He *was* my best friend . . ."

CHAPTER NINE

Archbishop Reilly's private chapel looked like a small courtroom. Most of the pews had been removed. The episcopal chair had been carried to the center of the platform on which the altar stood, and its plush, forbidding emptiness faced the few remaining benches. A small armchair had been placed on the floor to the right, also facing the pews, and opposite the chair, in front of the pews, were two large tables, one on the right and the other on the left, with a couple of chairs neatly facing the archbishop's chair. To the left, against the wall, there were two more chairs behind a smaller table. The dark wood paneling of the chapel lent the place a solemn atmosphere. The archbishop had thought that this was the ideal place to conduct the hearings, for the rules of procedure emphasized secrecy and directed that the court meet "in a sacred place."

The archbishop had decided to preside, and he had appointed himself chief judge, as was his prerogative, since the hearings were being held in his archdiocese. He had taken good care to select for the rest of the tribunal the very best people he could find. To this effect, he had appointed Father Berchman as postulator of the cause. His task would be to gather the necessary information and present the witnesses favorable to Morrison's cause. Father Berchman was a clever theologian with a doctorate in Canon Law (as the rules required). He was a professor at the Seminary and well respected in the archdiocese. Then, as promoter of the faith, commonly known as "devil's advocate," he had appointed Monsignor Olp, an older priest, head of one of the largest city parishes, a theologian of note with many scholarly articles to his credit, who also held the required doctorate in Canon Law. His task would be to examine the written depositions and documents and to interrogate the witnesses presented, to make sure that the truth of the matter was established beyond a reasonable doubt. In a way, the promoter's task was to ensure that the faith remained unsullied. For this, it was necessary to scrutinize any and all writings of the candidate for doctrinal orthodoxy, and to examine all the witnesses who could attest to the candidate's purity of morals. As if this were not enough, the promoter also had to ascertain the validity of claims that miracles had occurred through the intercession of the candidate, one of the most formidable tasks in a scientific and skeptical age. The rest of the tribunal included the archbishop's own secretary and a stenographer.

A couple of months before the start of the proceedings, the archbishop had mandated that proclamations be read in all the churches of the archdiocese, announcing the beginning of the process and calling anyone who knew Morrison personally to come forward to witness or to give a written deposition. Similarly, he had asked that anyone in possession of letters or other writings of Morrison's take them to the local parish priest to be photocopied or submitted in the original form as evidence.

All this was necessary as part of the information-gathering process, the first step toward canonization. It made sense that this preliminary step was taken at the local level, for the locale where the candidate had lived was the most likely to produce information relevant to the case. At the same time, such a place was most open to the pressures and connivance of interested parties. Therefore, most of the 142 canons that dealt with canonization concerned the constitution and procedures of the local tribunal, especially the very important matter of secrecy. For example, the procedures were to be strictly private, and the witnesses had to swear to keep their own testimony, as well as anything else they learned, totally to themselves. All the records were to be sealed at the end of each session, kept in a safe place, and reopened only at the beginning of the next session in the presence of all the court members and after careful inspection of the seals and verification of their integrity. Once this process was completed, the candidacy moved to Rome, where the Sacred Congregation of Rites took over the inquiry until its completion. Such had been the practice since 1634 when Pope

Urban VIII forbade the public cult of anyone not officially canonized.

The first meeting of the tribunal was taking place on a sunny, cold, mid-winter day. The sleeping ground was covered with a blanket of snow. Indoors, in the chapel, the cold of the night was responding to the heat of the radiators, but the chill had not disappeared completely. The chapel was well lighted, and the candles on the altar were burning steadily, spreading the smell of wax all around.

The archbishop walked in, dressed in all his finery, accompanied by the other members of the tribunal. They all stood at their places while the prelate administered to them the oath, which he also took. He intoned, "In the name of the Lord. Amen. I, John Reilly, by the grace of God, Archbishop of this Church, do solemnly swear to fulfill thoroughly all the duties pertaining to this task, to accept no gifts from any party related or not to these proceedings while this court is in session, and to keep secret whatever shall transpire in this court and whatever I shall read in the documents pertaining thereto. So help me God."

The secretary had written down the oath by hand in the registry, and each of the participants had signed his name upon the page, the secretary being the last. The secretary had then placed a drop of molten sealing wax on the page, and the archbishop had pressed on it his signet ring. When they had all returned to their chairs, the archbishop began:

"The first order of business is to inquire into the beginnings of these canonization proceedings and whether or not they should have been started before today. Since the death of the servant of God, William Morrison, occurred more than thirty years ago, the reasons for the delay must be ascertained."

The promoter rose from his seat and, looking at some papers spread on the table before him, said, "Your grace, it appears from the evidence submitted to me by the postulator, that your grace initiated an unofficial inquiry eleven years ago and followed it by obtaining a notarized deposition from a witness last year. Your grace, while there is no question of impugning your grace's conduct, the promoter believes it would be in the best interests of the case to hear directly from Mr. Jones."

"Indeed," the archbishop replied. "The postulator will see to it that Mr. Jones is called in to testify at our next session."

"Thank you, your grace," the promoter said and sat down.

"The next business," the archbishop began again, "is the matter of prior cult. The court must ascertain whether or not a public worship of William Morrison was ever instituted before this day. Do we have the necessary witnesses?"

"Yes, your grace," the postulator responded, rising from his seat. "They are outside awaiting instructions from your grace."

"Bring the first one in," the archbishop said.

Four witnesses were needed in this matter. One, the official in charge of the cemetery grounds, testified under oath that Morrison's tomb had not been a center of veneration, that no votive offerings or unusual flower displays had been noted, and that no crowds gathered there on the occasion of the anniversary of his death. The second, a neighbor and friend of the family for many years, was asked about signs of public interest centered on his birthplace in the Bronx or any of the apartments where the family had lived or where Morrison had died. To all these questions he had answered in the negative. Moreover, he added that Morrison's widow would have known if anything of the kind were happening, and that she had never mentioned such a thing to him.

"This would mean only that she didn't tell you," interrupted the monsignor, "not that it didn't happen."

"Ah . . . yes, sir," the witness replied. "That would be correct."

"Thank you," the monsignor concluded. "You may step down."

The other two witnesses, the priest in charge of the parish in which Morrison had lived all his life, and the editor of a local newspaper, also testified that, to their knowledge, there had never been any public veneration of Morrison.

At that point the postulator introduced into evidence two large boxfuls of letters received by the archdiocese requesting the canonization of Morrison. The letters, he said, contained no indication of worship. They were just petitions from the mighty, as well as the lowly, attesting to Morrison's sanctity and requesting his canonization. Monsignor Olp had acknowledged them and agreed that they contained no indication of public veneration. The act was recorded in the official proceedings.

This marked the end of the first session of the court. The transcripts were sealed and the meeting adjourned.

. . . .

Later that day, the archbishop found himself standing in front of the high window of his ninth-floor chancery office. He couldn't see much of the city from there, for the tall buildings and skyscrapers in the vicinity towered above the chancery, blocking the view. But, from this height, he could look down on the streets below, awash in the slush remaining from the morning snow; on the shops, cafes, and restaurants of the neighborhood; on the street vendors and the truckers delivering goods; on the traffic; and on the pedestrians wending their way through the crowds they themselves created. For a moment he felt isolated from it all: a minuscule snowflake fallen into an enormous ocean, conscious of its identity an instant before it ceased to be itself and merged forever with the elements; caught ineluctably in a never-ending pattern of dissolution, evaporation, rise, condensation and individuation, and fall. And here he was, during that brief span of time in which he was an individual self, with hardly a perspective at all on the world beyond the skyscrapers, purporting to inquire into the eternal fate of Morrison! The ludicrousness of his position broke in on him like a flash of lightning, and it was gone as quickly. He returned to his desk to get on with his work, but the momentary vision left a strange taste in his mouth, like a bit of licorice.

CHAPTER TEN

The court convened again a few days later. After some brief announcements, Jones was ushered in, walked to the witness stand and was sworn in, after which he sat down. Monsignor Olp began by inquiring if Archbishop Reilly had asked him to look into the details of Morrison's life.

"Yes," answered Jones.

"Why did he ask you to do that?" the monsignor continued.

"Because he had been receiving letters requesting Morrison's canonization," Jones replied.

"What did you find?" queried the promoter.

"Not much beyond what was generally known from the biographers."

"Did you contact the biographers?"

"I tried to," Jones explained, "but two of them were dead and the third had Alzheimer's disease. I did speak to Morrison's widow, but she didn't have anything significant to say."

At this point Father Berchman, the postulator, interrupted.

"There is no need of extraordinary evidence in order to begin a fact-finding inquiry," he said to the court. "Canon 2050, paragraph 2, says that very clearly."

"Read the canon in question," the archbishop ordered the secretary.

The secretary thumbed through a thick volume containing the code of Canon Law, and then read:

> It is not necessary to have specific evidence of virtue, martyrdom, and miracles; it is enough to prove that there is a general and spontaneous reputation, not contrived by human effort, held by honest and serious persons, continuous and actually increasing from day to day, to be found among a majority of the people.

"I am not after miracles here," the promoter said after the secretary had finished. "I merely want to ascertain the course of events."

"Proceed," the archbishop directed.

"Thank you, your grace," the monsignor said. Then, addressing Jones again, he inquired, "Did you contact any other witnesses?"

"Yes, sir," Jones answered, "one more."

"The name?"

"Miss Julie Carter, the actress."

"How many times did you meet her?"

"Twice, the second time almost a year ago."

"Why did you seek her a second time?"

"To get a written statement from her." Jones paused briefly. "Her statement has been submitted as evidence."

"I'm aware of that, Mr. Jones," the monsignor said, "though I have yet to see the point of it." He looked at his papers, before addressing Jones once more. "At any rate, you can testify to the effect that his grace directed you to seek information relevant to Morrison's cause, in effect beginning the investigative process?"

"That's correct," Jones replied.

"So there's no doubt in your mind that his grace intended to begin this process, and that his asking you to investigate was part of the preliminaries?"

Jones thought for a moment of his discussions with the archbishop regarding the matter of canonization, but he felt that they were not relevant to the question asked. What seemed important was the fact that his friend had asked him to look for information regarding Morrison's relationship with the actress.

"No, there's no doubt," he answered.

"Thank you, Mr. Jones," the monsignor said. "Please remain seated," he added, as he jotted something down on a note pad and looked unhurriedly through some papers. When he spoke again he looked directly at the archbishop.

"Your grace," he said, "the promoter is satisfied that the investigation was begun within the thirty years specified by Canon Law. Even though this court was not convened within that period, a reasonable investigation was started nonetheless, as would have been required by this court anyway. There is no need to dally on this point."

"The secretary shall so note," the archbishop directed.

The promoter looked through some more papers and then addressed the archbishop again.

"Your grace," he said, "if the court has no objection, I'd like to proceed to question Mr. Jones about more substantive matters." He paused, looking at his notes. "The first one," he continued, "concerns Morrison's writings." Then, addressing Jones, he asked, "Mr. Jones, you have taught classical literature for many years. What is your considered estimate of Morrison's poetry?"

Jones leaned back on the chair while he prepared to answer. He recalled briefly the time, some twelve years before, when he had first read Morrison's published works. At that time, he had been concerned with their content, mystical and sexual, not with their literary quality. He had been trying to determine whether or not the mysticism was genuine, and whether it was sullied by the sexual content, as some thought, or, rather, was unaffected by it. The critique he was being asked to make now was different, and yet, he thought, not really so.

"Contemporary literary criticism, as you know," he began, "is rather complex. It seldom—"

"We needn't get into scholarly controversy, Mr. Jones," Monsignor Olp interrupted. "Just a simple appraisal."

"But that *is* the point," Jones retorted unfazed. "Evaluation itself determines the value of the piece. In fact, reading affects our judgment of a work of literature. For example, the more extensively read an author is, the more worthy of being read the work becomes. This is a factor that cannot be ignored. On the other hand, who the readers are and what they are looking for are also matters of importance. We construct meaning, Father. We do not merely *find* it."

"But such matters aside," the promoter insisted, "what is your judgment of the literary merit of Morrison's work?"

"That judgment has been expressed by many," answered Jones. "My view is not novel or original. Morrison's work is solid, well crafted . . . for the most part. It is inspired, both in the traditional sense as well as in the more religious or spiritual meaning. After all, a lot of his poetry was mystical in nature."

Monsignor Olp was looking at the papers spread in front of him on the table. He didn't seem to be paying attention to Jones's explanation. When Jones finished speaking, the Monsignor didn't look up. An awkward silence followed, mercifully broken by the president.

"He wasn't this century's greatest poet, was he?" the archbishop asked.

"No, your grace," Jones responded, looking at his friend. "Morrison was a competent, often inspired poet. Many of his poems were lyrical. I have often thought that if typewriters were pianos, such poems would have been songs."

"So you admit he was mediocre?" asked the promoter, suddenly coming to life again.

"No," replied Jones, turning toward him. "I didn't say that."

"What *did* you say, Mr. Jones?"

"I said that he was a competent poet—a good poet, if you like."

"And that judgment applies also to his sexual poetry, would you say?"

"Indeed," Jones said, somewhat taken aback by the shift from form to content.

"Mr. Jones," Monsignor Olp intoned tendentiously, "do you mean to tell us that the sexuality of Morrison's poetry is not relevant to an evaluation of its literary merit?"

"That's correct," answered Jones.

"But why would anyone write such . . . stuff?" the monsignor insisted.

"Sexuality, like beauty, is a construct, Father. We interpret what was written, claiming to discover in the words the meaning intended by the poet." Jones cleared his throat, then added, "How can we be sure of Morrison's intent? All we have are his words!"

"And his love of God," interjected Father Berchman.

"Indeed," rejoined the promoter rather testily. He obviously had not relished the innuendo. "But I want to know what you think of his sexual poetry, especially when taken in the context of his alleged mysticism."

"I see no problem with that at all," answered Jones. "I am aware of the fact that traditional views of mystical love have tended to ignore the physical dimensions. But one need only recollect the *Song of Songs* to realize that the ecstasies of love can be divine as well as fleshly."

"I know the argument," Monsignor Olp said, implying he didn't want to proceed in that direction. But Jones did go on.

"Surely, you remember Saint Theresa of Avila and the complex sexual metaphors that shrouded her rapturous communion with God. And Thomas Merton, the mystical Cistercian, who, in the throes of sexual love, could write about the print of M's breasts upon his heart, and confess how, 'In the night when nothing can be seen I turn / To my Beloved and her voice is my security.'"

"Enough, Mr. Jones," the monsignor said impatiently. "No need to get carried away."

"Elijah was whisked away in a chariot of fire, Father," Jones replied with some feeling, "not in an ice bucket."

The archbishop smiled inwardly at his friend's words, but said nothing. Monsignor Olp was shuffling again through his papers, as if nothing had happened.

"Mr. Jones, after your first inquiry, you concluded that Morrison was a saint. Is that correct?"

"Yes," replied Jones.

"Is this your position still?"

"Yes, Father."

"In your letter to his grace, you gave no reasons for your statement. What grounds did you have for your judgment?"

Jones thought for a few moments, then replied, "The essence of sanctity is possession by the divine." He paused briefly. "To be possessed, the human soul must be opened to the divine indwelling like a room to the rays of the morning sun. Such openness is the work of the imagination—"

"Isn't it the work of grace?" interrupted the promoter.

"Indeed," said Jones gesticulating slowly as he searched for the right words, sensing he had to be precise. He was somewhat out of his depth here and was relying on shreds of memories from his studies at seminary a long time ago. "But grace presupposes the willingness to receive, which in turn requires that we see ourselves as unfilled receptacles . . . as unfinished beings . . . as not being what we can be. Of course, God helps in all of this. As Saint Augustine says—"

"I know what Saint Augustine says," Monsignor Olp interrupted curtly. "The point is that God would not inspire thoughts of sex, much less of illicit sex, especially in a married man, would he?" He looked over his notes as if he were following a prepared script. "Images of extra-marital sex are sinful, Mr. Jones, as I'm sure you know—"

"Sexual thoughts are sexual thoughts," Jones muttered under his breath.

"What was that?" asked the promoter, obviously annoyed at the interruption. "If your comment is relevant, it must be said loud enough to be recorded."

"I said that sexual thoughts are just like any other thoughts," replied Jones. "Labeling them sinful is a construct, Father."

"But an appropriate one here, wouldn't you say? After all, we're dealing with sanctity."

"Look," said Jones, "millions of people have sexual thoughts . . . and thoughts of food, pain, comfort, jealousy, kindness, and unkindness, yet their souls are open to the divine benevolence. Isn't this the most important thing? Isn't the openness the thing that matters, regardless of the content?"

"Mr. Jones," the promoter replied, "the faith I'm sworn to uphold declares otherwise."

"'Love and do what you will,' isn't that what Saint Augustine said?" pleaded Jones.

The promoter didn't reply right away. He looked at his notes; it was clear that he did that whenever he needed to think, as a way of gaining time to choose his words.

"Mr. Jones," he said finally, "canonizing someone means that the person is in heaven and that the life led on earth is worthy of imitation. Are we justified in claiming that a man who writes of sexual desires about a woman not his wife is worthy of imitation?"

"But is that all?" asked Jones in disbelief. "Is this all you can see in Morrison's life?"

"A saint's life must be pure through and through," replied the monsignor. "I'm not saying he's not saved. I'm saying he's not worthy of being prayed to, not worthy of being imitated."

"But thousands of people have thought otherwise," intervened Father Berchman. "Their letters clearly indicate this."

"The point is whether we should sanction their thoughts," replied the promoter.

"Are you suggesting that this inquiry should end?" asked the archbishop.

"No, your grace," the promoter answered, "at least not yet. The time may come for that. I'm saying that we cannot ignore or gloss over some facts in this case that have to do with sex . . . with sexual harassment."

"No such charge was ever filed against Morrison," the postulator insisted. "It doesn't seem fair to drag that into this inquiry."

"This is a *fact*-finding inquiry, I remind you," the promoter stated curtly. "All facts are relevant until proven otherwise."

"But isn't this what Mr. Jones set out to find the first time around? Whether or not there had been sexual harassment?" asked the postulator.

"Indeed," the promoter replied with a hint of annoyance in his voice. "And what did he find?" he asked, addressing himself to Jones.

"That she had *not* charged him, though at the time she felt there had been harassment," answered Jones. "But ten years later, she had changed her mind because she was confronted with a different possibility."

"But left to herself, she would have maintained her initial position, wouldn't she?" insisted the promoter. "That's what she had told the biographers."

"Perhaps," replied Jones, "but you yourself, if you had been questioning her, would have suggested the possibility of other interpretations, at least in order to ascertain the degree of her conviction. And shouldn't we take as her true opinion that contained in her deposition? After all, she could have insisted that her old views were the true ones, yet she changed her mind on her own."

"As the result of your prodding, Mr. Jones," said the promoter, "as the result of your prodding."

"But I didn't see or speak to the woman for ten years," Jones exclaimed. "Surely, no matter what I said, she had enough time to make up her own mind."

"Then perhaps we should hear from the woman herself," the postulator suggested. "Your grace," he continued quickly, addressing the president, "I respectfully request that Miss Carter be invited to testify in this court."

"I so order," the archbishop ruled. Then, addressing the promoter, he asked: "Do you have any more questions for the witness?"

"No, your grace," the promoter replied.

"Mr. Jones," the archbishop addressed his friend, "thank you for your testimony. You may step down."

. . . .

That evening, in his study, the archbishop sat at his desk and leaned back in his chair. Closing his eyes, he pondered the events of the day, and the matter before him and the court. Was Morrison really a saint? Was that at all significant? What did saintliness have to do with sexuality? What did it take to be a saint? Why was sainthood considered the acme of human achievement? What did one really accomplish when one became a saint? Could one really *become* a saint? He could describe the characteristics of the lives of people who had been labeled saints. They had been pious, humble, prudent, ascetical, generous, loving, and so forth. But, combined, all these virtues simply described a type of human being. He knew of people—not too many, to be sure—who possessed all those qualities and had cultivated them in their lives, yet would never be called saints. Gandhi, surely, had had them all, and yet he was not deemed a saint. At least not by the Church. He also felt that becoming a saint was not something you could *do*. It was something that was done to you by your friends, your fellow monks, members of your family, co-religionists, and the like. That's why it always happened *after* you were dead, when there was nothing you could *do* about it.

He wondered if saints did what they did for the sake of becoming saints or just to be what they thought they had to be, in the presence of God, of course, but not necessarily in the presence of the Church. St. Ignatius was someone he knew of who had set out to become a saint, fired by the example of the lives of the saints he had read while convalescing from his war wounds. But surely, what he had set out to do was imitate the deeds of their lives, perhaps enticed by the prospect of glory and renown associated with the title. But it wouldn't have taken too long to realize that the halo was affixed posthumously. It was like a stamp of approval set upon a life already lived. But *what* the life was had been determined already, irrevocably, before canonization proceedings could even start.

It struck him that being a saint had less to do with being a good person than with being noticed by the right people. God saw everyone, but the Church saw only those it wished to see or those it was forced to see by political or other pressures. And it was only these people it saw that were labeled saints.

So why had he been striving to become a saint? Why had he asked his friend Jones, some twelve or thirteen years before, whether or not he was a saint? Why was that important if it didn't depend on him, if it was something bestowed, and arbitrarily at that? Perhaps this was the reason he and his friend were so unsure about the whole process, even though he had started the proceedings. There was something artificial about the inquiry. Why wasn't one instead concerned with ascertaining whether or not people had led a *good* life, whether or not they had cared for others, endured their lot with patience, and laughed in the face of pain and rejection? Surely, *this* could be ascertained, but *sainthood*?

He opened his eyes and looked at his watch. It was late, so he decided to say his evening prayers and retire for the night. He opened à Kempis and read:

> "Do not inquire or dispute concerning the merits of the saints . . . Curiosity about such matters and inquiry into them are unprofitable. For God says: I embrace all alike with an inestimable love. They are all one through the bond of charity; their thoughts are the same; their will is the same; and they are all united in love, one for another, and for Me, wherein they rest in the fruition of their love."

For a minute or two the archbishop pondered the wisdom of the old writer from Kempen. As his mind dwelled peacefully on the passage he had just read, he remembered that the scripture for the day had contained the words of Jesus, "You have my Father's blessing; come, enter and possess the kingdom. For when I was hungry, you gave me food; when thirsty, you gave me drink; when I was a stranger you took me into your home, when naked you clothed me; when I was ill you came to my help, when in prison you visited me." All these were deeds, he thought, ordinary deeds such as anyone could perform, and yet, because of them, the doers were being blessed and ushered into the kingdom.

He meditated some more upon the scriptures. Then he rose from his chair, turned off his desk lamp, and walked slowly to his bedroom.

CHAPTER ELEVEN

The phone rung early one morning, a few days after Jones had given testimony. He picked up the receiver and said quietly, "Hello?"

"Mr. Jones?" a woman queried on the other end. "This is Julie Carter. . . . How are you?"

"Miss Carter?"

"Yes, Mr. Jones, the very selfsame. I hope you're not in the middle of something. I realize it's quite early." She paused and Jones assured her that she had not disturbed him. She proceeded, "I have been invited to go down to New York to testify in Bill's case, and I was wondering . . . could you pick me up at La Guardia? I haven't been to the city in years, and I'd rather meet someone I know there."

"Of course," answered Jones. "I'd be delighted. How often am I asked to escort a beautiful lady into town?"

"Oh, cut it out," she said, laughing.

She gave him the particulars of her arrival, and he told her how much he was looking forward to seeing her again, this time in his own territory. With that, the conversation ended.

Jones thought of calling his friend, Archbishop Reilly, to chat about Miss Carter's impending visit, but he realized they both were sworn to secrecy in matters pertaining to the case, so there wasn't much they could talk about. He decided to keep his thoughts to himself, at least this once. Not that he anticipated any trouble, he was simply concerned about Miss Carter, and he felt he bore a certain responsibility for whatever discomfort she might encounter. After all, he had been the one to track her down.

A few days later, Jones picked up Miss Carter at the airport and drove her to her hotel in Manhattan. The archbishop's secretary had made all the arrangements for her, and he must have insisted she be given special attention, for she was greeted with utmost courtesy. Jones accompanied her to her room, tipped the bellboy, and helped her a little with her things. He then excused himself, promising to come back later to take her out to dinner.

"I'll be looking forward to that," she said as he left her room on the way to the elevators.

Back in his own apartment, he telephoned La Reserve to make dinner reservations for two.

. . . .

Jones returned to the hotel at around six that evening, called Miss Carter on the intercom, and waited for her in the lobby.

"Good evening, Mr. Jones," he heard her say, and he turned to meet her.

She walked toward him with regal step, her presence exuding charm. Her purse was hanging from her left shoulder, and both arms were extended toward him with hands palm up. Jones placed his hands in hers and gently kissed her mouth.

"You look stunning tonight. This must have brought back memories."

"Indeed!" she replied.

She was wearing a light blue dress that matched as closely as possible the color of her beautiful eyes. The skirt was full, and it reached below her knees. A brilliant pendant, hanging from a gold chain around her neck, was poised on her chest slightly below the top of the dress. A dark blue jacket completed her outfit and provided contrast to her white, silky hair, which was worn simply: straight and short. A solitary diamond adorned each ear.

He offered her his arm, and they left the hotel. In a short while, they were sitting at a table in the restaurant, sipping sherry and conversing intimately. The restaurant was not crowded. The quiet hum of polite conversation contributed to a feeling of peace and relaxation, and a sense that the evening could be spent in unhurried tribute to their growing friendship.

"The mind is an amazing thing," she was telling Jones after they placed their orders. "It can obliterate existence. It can deny that something happened, or forget it did, or remember it very differently from the way it happened. And yet our minds are the past's only hope."

"Why are you saying that?" he inquired.

"I was remembering what happened after my break with Bill. Months after we parted, I could still accuse Bill of expecting from me feelings and considerations I assured him I didn't have . . . and claimed I had never had." She sipped some sherry, then wiped her mouth lightly with the napkin. "I accused him of misreading things, of seeing in my actions intentions I had never had. I maintained that I had never given him grounds for making such interpretations. But you know, I *had* given him grounds."

"What do you mean?"

"Well," she answered, leaning back in her chair while keeping her right hand on the base of her glass of sherry, "for instance, at some point we had talked about our feelings for each other. We compared them with feelings we had had toward others, relatives and friends. I told Bill quite clearly where he stood with me. I compared my affection for him to that which I had had for a favorite uncle of mine and for another friend. I had told him he was my friend. And here I was, after the break, accusing him of harassing me because he expected me to act toward him like a friend. Isn't that strange?"

"I hear you saying that you had given him clear indications that he was your friend, at least before—"

"Sure I had," she interrupted, before quickly adding, "Sorry for cutting you off!"

"Not at all," he responded. "Please, go on."

"I told him . . . actually, I had *written* to him how much I cared for him."

"*Cared*," he emphasized, "not *loved* . . . I remember the distinction."

"Right. I had *written* to him, yet there I was, after the break, denying it all, pretending it had not happened, complaining that he was expecting from me what I couldn't give him, when actually, for a time, I had given him my love."

"*Care*, that is," Jones interposed again.

"Sure . . . right," she agreed.

"Basically, you were deconstructing your past—that's what we say nowadays, you know," he said with a smile. He paused briefly to take a sip from his glass. "It's like saying the past never happened because you can't determine any more what you felt, what you said, or what you meant."

She paid no heed to his comment, but continued on the path she had already started. "That must have driven Bill crazy," she said.

"Why?"

"Well," she replied, sitting up straight and then leaning forward slightly to get closer to him, as if she were afraid of being overheard. "I think Bill thought the world of me. Modesty aside, I believe he thought I was wonderful. And not because of the films."

"No," Jones interjected. "From what I know of him, he was not taken up by glamor and glitter."

"No, not at all," she continued. "He knew that the glamor was part of acting and promotional exaggeration. He had seen through all that. But my feelings, my sensibilities, my views on life, my values, my intelligence, my beauty—all these appealed to him. He felt we were very much alike, and I agreed. I kept saying to him, 'We're so much alike!' every time we shared comments, inklings, and assessments of people and situations."

"I can see how that would have been endearing."

"And to know himself loved by me . . . you see, that must have made him feel his life was justified, validated. This kindred soul," she said, pointing to herself, "cared for him."

"Exactly."

She fell silent for a while. By this time, their meal had been served, and she nibbled at it pensively, almost in a desultory fashion, though the food was exquisite and the presentation dainty. Jones did not feel like prodding. He was very relaxed and willing to take whatever the next moment would bring.

"You know, Mr. Jones," she said, finally breaking the silence, "when I was a little girl in school in Arkansas, my second grade teacher, Mrs. Walker—I can still see the dear old lady!—gave me a prize for something I had done . . . done well, I suppose, though I don't remember what it was. Then, at the end of class, she took it away from me. I don't know why. To this day, I don't know why she took my prize away. But that's precisely what I did to Bill. I took *his* prize away without telling him why." She paused briefly. "Bill was a good man, Mr. Jones. I wish you had known him."

"I wish I had, too."

"Being called a friend by me was like proof that he had taken the right path through life. It was like finding a treasure at the end of years of seeking, or like finding the solution to a riddle after years of painful inquiry. And now, when he had his validation—his proof, as it were—I was taking it all away from him. I was pulling the rug from under his feet by saying that none of it had really happened."

"You are saying," Jones ventured tentatively, "that the supposed harassment was not the real reason you broke up the friendship. Isn't that so?"

"Yes, yes," she replied eagerly. "That's why, even then, I didn't accuse him of sexual harassment. Even at that time, I had a feeling—just a feeling, you know, something really profound and unfathomable—that something else was making me reject him. I didn't know for sure what it was, and I would not discuss the situation with Bill. So, essentially, I was denying myself the opportunity of finding out."

"And denying it to him, too," Jones added.

"Indeed."

"Also," Jones continued, "this means that you never quite gave him a reason for your rejection."

"That's the truth," she agreed, sadly. She paused for a few minutes, fixing her eyes on the tablecloth absently. "That's the truth," she repeated pensively, shaking her head quietly. "I rejected him, gave him no reason, and forbade him to inquire."

"And yet, he continued to love you and to hope—"

"Until his death," she interrupted. "Until his very death," she made a vague gesture of frustration with her hand, "like a spurned puppy who knows only to be loyal and wait for his mistress's love."

Their dinner was almost over. The French pastries for dessert were light and delicious, and the warmth of the coffee contributed to the feeling of repose that had pervaded the entire evening.

While she was stirring her coffee slowly, as if she were readying a strange elixir, she looked at Jones directly.

"Mr. Jones, I presume you are Roman Catholic."

Jones nodded affirmatively.

"This is not meant as . . . I can't find the word, but neither Bill nor I believed in confession . . . you know, to a priest. That's why we confessed to each other all the secrets of our lives . . . freely, you know. We never questioned each other. We simply told each other our inmost thoughts and deeds, and in the hearing, we were each other's pardon. That is, if one needs absolution for just living. You understand, don't you?"

"Yes. I think I do."

"Thank you," she said.

With that, they got up and left the restaurant. They returned to the hotel, and Jones accompanied her to her room. As he was taking leave of her, informing her that he would call on her again the next day, Miss Carter took his hands firmly in hers, looked lovingly, or perhaps longingly, into his eyes, and, with a touch of mischief in her voice, said:

"Mr. Jones, thank you for hearing my confession tonight."

CHAPTER TWELVE

The next morning, Miss Carter walked into the courtroom, took the oath of secrecy, and sat down. Besides her pocketbook, she was carrying a small briefcase. From her seat, she eyed the chapel that was serving as courtroom and took note of the various participants seated at their tables.

After a few preliminaries, the promoter began his questioning. First of all, he said, he wanted to know if she and Morrison had been friends.

"Yes, of course," she replied with a smile. "We were very close friends. Everybody knew that, and his biographers have given testimony to that effect."

"Did he express his friendship to you? I mean," he explained, "did he tell you explicitly that you were his friend?"

"Yes, sir."

"What was special about your friendship?"

"Well, sir," she offered, "to begin with, we liked each other. This is hard to explain, but we felt completely at ease with each other from the moment we met. Then we grew to trust each other implicitly. With the greatest ease, we would volunteer information about ourselves without being asked. We flowed into each other like breezes blowing playfully on a sunny summer afternoon."

"What accounted for your friendship?" the promoter asked. "I mean, how did it begin?"

"We were introduced to each other before a talk show. We had the same agent."

"Had you met before?"

"No, sir, we hadn't. I seem to recollect that he said he had seen one of my movies, or maybe two. That was the extent of it. But when our eyes met that afternoon, something else happened beyond the mere formalities of introductions—a sort of feeling of connection, as if our souls were wired and a switch had just been thrown." She looked around quickly and nervously. "It's almost funny, but what would a magnet and a piece of iron say of their first encounter?"

She looked around again as if expecting some acknowledgment, but knowing there would be none. Then her eyes shifted to one side, and with a vacant look she continued.

"Perhaps better, it was as if we were what each had always wanted in a friend. And, in that moment, we were discovering it for the first time. Even though we had just been introduced, there was a sense of recognition that would only grow at each successive meeting."

She looked at the promoter, who was shuffling papers, ostensibly paying no heed to her words.

She ventured to add, "It's as if we had known each other intimately for years, and had just picked up our friendship again where we had left off."

"Did he write about your friendship?" the promoter inquired.

"Indeed," she replied. "He wrote several poems about our friendship. If I could take a look at his collected poems, I'm sure I could easily find one or two."

"Will you please hand Miss Carter the book of Morrison's poetry?" the archbishop asked the secretary.

She took the book and leafed through it quickly, looking knowingly for a specific place and then finding it.

"This is one of his later sonnets, written while we were appearing on talk shows together. Shall I read part of it at least?"

"Yes, please read as much as you want," directed the president.

She cleared her throat and read:

Let them their ignorance betray
Who ask what found I in your noble self . . .
O foolish world! It knows not what is worth,
And shining bits it thus for gold mistakes
When measuring our worth by noble birth
Or by our wits, while other gifts forsakes.
Ten times I too did search, ten times I erred
And struck no golden vein or river bed;

Perhaps it was my eyes that were too blurred
To see the splendor the true metal shed.
    But I did search for gold, and gold I found,
    And ascertained, to you myself I bound.

"That's just one poem." She raised her eyes from the book slowly, with a wistful look on her face. "There are others, and there is, of course, the *Elegies*."

"Thank you," the promoter said. "That'll do for now."

He looked through his papers for a minute, then said he wanted to know if Morrison had written to her.

"Yes, sir," she answered, closing the book that had remained open in her hands all this time. The secretary rose from his seat and took the book from her. "He did write to me both before and after the incident. Some of the letters were innocuous and, therefore, I didn't keep them. Of the others, I have made photocopies that I'd be glad to leave with you." She opened her briefcase and took out a few sheets of paper, saying, "The only one I did not copy was the note that Pickering mentioned in his introduction to the *Elegies*. The text is exactly as he reported it. After all," she added with a wan smile, "I showed him the original."

"Could you tell us briefly what is contained in them?" the promoter asked.

"Sure," she replied, shuffling through the papers. "There is a poem he wrote shortly before we parted. He sent me this handwritten copy, and the poem was never published. It is based on a comment I had once made to him, which seems to have fused into a dream."

The dream:

> Two-tiered vision—
>
> Jocular at first
> Upon first entering your room:
> You won't denude yourself as usual,
> As you said you do,
> To rest, exhausted from the day's work.
>
> Next,
> Twined naked forms in bed,
> Your head upon my breast
> Chastely comforting.
>
> Such peace—

"Did you find it offensive?" the promoter inquired.

"Not really," she answered, "though I think I blushed at the time."

"Was Morrison ever in your home?" he persisted.

"No, sir," she replied curtly.

After the briefest of pauses, which could have been read as a slight hesitation, the promoter continued, "Anything else?"

"Well, yes," she answered, gathering the papers once more and offering them to him. "Take a look yourself. There is nothing really special."

The promoter walked around the table, took the sheets, and eyed them quickly as he returned to his place.

"Anything *after* you parted?"

"Yes," she said, unperturbed. "Besides the note mentioned by Pickering, there's a brief paragraph. It's on the last page. It says simply, 'I'm striving to be the best gift I could ever offer you. Please be assured that I have never felt for you anything but the purest love of friendship.' As you can tell," she added, "I have memorized it."

"Yes, indeed you have," the promoter murmured with a shrug, having scanned the last page as she spoke. "Why didn't you mention these notes to the biographers?"

"Because even an actress is entitled to some privacy," she replied with some feeling.

The promoter paid no attention to her comment. His interests seemed to be purely legalistic.

"Your relationship with Morrison ended due to an unfortunate incident, isn't that so?"

"Yes, sir," she replied with a faint tone of apprehension in her voice. "I'd say there was a misunderstanding between us."

"Could you please explain?"

"Of course. Actually, it was something he said to me. . . . I misunderstood—"

"What did he say to you?" the monsignor asked, staring at her.

"He said . . . he would have liked very much to make love to me," she replied, meeting his stare. Closing her eyes, she crossed her left arm over her stomach and, resting the elbow of her right arm on it, covered her mouth with her right hand.

For a brief moment, Monsignor Olp showed that he cared about the pain and embarrassment she was obviously experiencing, lowering his eyes and allowing Miss Carter to collect herself while he looked fixedly at the papers on the table. When he spoke again, the tone of his voice was discernibly lower and even considerate.

"Is that the reason why you charged him with sexual harassment?" he asked.

She uncovered her mouth but did not open her eyes.

"I didn't accuse him of anything," she said deliberately, "although at the time I thought I could have. His behavior seemed patently provocative—a sexual invitation, if there ever was one. But I didn't want to hurt him . . . though, in fact, I spared his public image at the expense of his soul." She stopped. "I hurt him," she concluded sadly.

"What else could you have done?" asked the monsignor.

"I could have taken a broader view of the situation," she responded, opening her eyes, but not really speaking to him or even looking in his direction. Her words seemed addressed to no one in particular. "I could have taken his words as whim, as fancy, as what he would have liked to happen had he been unmarried and free, and I willing. Mr. Jones was right. By this time, Bill had told me everything about himself, every bit of his reality. The only thing left to share with me was his fantasy. Knowing his imagination would have given me possession of what he was and what he would have liked to be—of his past, present, and also his future.

"At that moment, when he confided his dreams to me, I owned him wholly. But I foolishly squandered my riches—what he had given me. I panicked. I abhorred his fantasy, selfishly, because it might have involved me. I refused him his future even before death robbed him of it. In fact," she added, becoming a bit agitated, "I became the executioner of his dreams."

The archbishop was leaning forward slightly, following her monologue with great attention. He seemed enthralled by the re-enactment of her tragedy, hearing for the first time the story that, until then, he had known only secondhand.

"I didn't get to know this until later," she went on, "many years later, when Mr. Jones re-interpreted Bill's words for me. At least, he presented another possibility I couldn't entirely reject, though I pretended I could."

"What interpretation was that?" asked the promoter.

"That I had turned his fantasy into reality," she replied. "I can admit that now, as I did in my deposition."

"Has this view changed since then?" the monsignor inquired.

"Not at all," she answered, "though I have come to see the whole episode in a still brighter light. You see, you don't know this, but in the warm womb of our friendship, Bill had entered upon a new road to self-knowledge—at least one he was not used to or had not traversed for quite a long time." She paused, and then, with some conviction, continued, "Bill was coming to understand himself as he never had before. He was becoming aware of the subtlest of connections between incidents in his past and of the effects they had had upon his life. In a very true sense, he was being reborn."

Her manner had become quite animated, almost anxious. In the courtroom, all eyes were riveted on her as if drawn by a special magnetism.

"He would have liked to make love to me, that's what he said . . . to the woman he fancied he would have liked to love above any other, and I took that realistically. But entering her was a metaphor for being reborn. You know, 'Unless one be born again . . .'

"I'm sure he knew this," she continued. "He even wrote a poem about it. My rejection threatened to make him an abortion and to leave him an incomplete being, a monstrosity dangling in the middle of nowhere." She leaned forward. "So he fought back with the only weapon he knew, his imagination. He wrote the *Elegies*—the latter parts, the poems of disillusion, despair, and, above all, hope."

Her voice trailed off a bit as she spoke those last words, and she closed her eyes again, leaning back in her chair. She looked tired after the emotional ordeal of summoning to the present the restless ghosts of so many feelings wandering the expanses of her past.

For a minute, nobody spoke. Then as if that brief respite had given her enough time to regain her strength, she continued, but her whole expression had changed. There was a sweet smile on her face, a glow, a sense of peace that radiated and spread, as it were, astride her words.

"Few things in the world could ever have been as beautiful as our friendship was. We spied with eagerness each other's moves, anticipated our arrivals, and watched each other come and go. Our faces lit up every time we met. We were immensely happy. We joked, we laughed, we talked, we went for strolls. We walked barefoot in the snow. We told each other our deepest thoughts and exchanged intimacies unasked." She lingered lovingly on the feelings wrapped around the thoughts. Then, as if returning from a dream journey, went on, "Friendship is mutual love. We were stars in each other's galaxies and alternately soloists in each other's orchestras.

"It is difficult to speak of what is wonderful in life." She smiled as she surveyed those present. "We lack the words for such glory, which is why people project their dreams of happiness to heaven, 'where the eye hath not seen.' But that time, for us, heaven was here on earth. Or, perhaps, for a while, some magic had transported us to an enchanted land where time dissolved and barriers dropped and love could be exchanged. Our friendship was as pure as a May morning in the sun, as peaceful as a moonlit night. And then," her voice became somber, "suddenly, without warning, it all ended, like a dream broken by a thunderclap.

"He made desperate attempts to regain the pristine beauty we both had enjoyed, to re-enter paradise. He struggled to save for us both what we both were losing, but I blocked his path like an angel with a flaming sword. I retreated into my own pain, forgetting or denying all that had been said and heard and felt and done—all, everything—forbidding him to salvage our sinking boat. I knew how badly he wanted to regain the paradise that was being lost, but I would have none of it. I spoke to him as if my memory had been wiped clean of any and all remembrances of our love.

"When he asked for a chance to explain himself, I replied that I was tired of listening, when in fact I hadn't listened at all. I avoided being alone with him. If our agent left the room, I would find some reason to get up and leave, as if I really feared he would come on to me. I must have thought that if I stayed away from him long enough, his lust would cease and he would stop loving me. Little did I suspect the strength and purity of his love. Really," she added, raising her eyes and looking slowly around the room, "he was proving to me how much he loved me, but I was so single-mindedly intent on denying him that I just couldn't see it." She heaved a deep sigh. "How this must have pained him! How he must have loved me, to endure the pain I was inflicting on him! I was hurting, too, for I was striving to stifle the love I felt for him, which I didn't have the strength to recognize and accept. . . . I was denying a part of me . . . but this was my way of dealing with my pain. I knew that he knew I was hurting, and that seeing me pained was torture, and a greater torture still not to be able to console me, for I had forbidden him. It must have felt like seeing your lover raped before your very eyes, your hands tied . . . his heart bound by his promise to me to abide."

She leaned back again, spent. Closing her eyes, she murmured, "Ah, the pity of it all! The pity . . . the slow, relentless martyrdom."

Monsignor Olp looked at her without raising his head. After a little while, he asked carefully, almost casually, "Therefore, do you agree he was a saint?"

"No!" she exclaimed, suddenly coming to life. "He was *not* a saint," she repeated emphatically. "Why do you want to rob him of his self, the self he fought for so tenaciously?" She calmed down a little. "Sainthood is something *you* bestow," she added with feeling, "something *you* determine for him. It's not something he could have *earned.*" The pace of her speech picked up slightly. "Bill knew that, and that's why he was not interested in sainthood but in friendship, in loving and becoming lovable . . . *making* himself lovable—that is, making himself the best gift he could be . . . *for me*, not for some nameless multitude of the faithful who had never known him, who would never care to know him, who could not reciprocate his love and become his friends. I turned him down because . . . because I couldn't comprehend this at the time. I couldn't deal with it, but I know now that this is the truth, the truth of Bill Morrison's life, the truth I am today trying, belatedly, to preserve."

The archbishop had sat back. His arms were resting on the arms of the chair, and his eyes were closed. Her long hymn to friendship was resounding in the temple of his spirit like the majestic chords of a great organ. Her words were washing over his soul like the waters of a curative spring over an aching limb.

The postulator had been startled by her vehemence and the message her words carried and was looking at the promoter inquiringly. The promoter, with an obvious show of disinterest, was busy gathering the papers on his table. He didn't seem in any hurry to respond. Perhaps he sensed with greater certainty what the others vaguely feared: that the inquiry into Morrison's sanctity was over and that there was nothing more to say. As the seconds ticked, the silence became unbearable. At long last the promoter spoke, addressing the archbishop. His voice was calm and his tone betrayed no emotion.

"Your grace," he said, "I respectfully request that these proceedings be closed and that this court be adjourned *sine die*."

Without opening his eyes, the archbishop replied softly, "So let it be written. So let it be done. In the name of the Lord. Amen."

CHAPTER THIRTEEN

Back in Waterville, Miss Carter was getting ready for bed. Her days after the hearing had been exhausting, not only because of the physical strain of moving about in the hurried surroundings of the bustling big city, but also, perhaps especially, because of the emotions she carried with her, weighing her down like heavy baggage. Even though Jones had endeavored to lighten her load and make her stay pleasant, the daily wear and tear had taken their toll, and she had felt increasingly tired, so that she had been relieved to leave and return to the slower pace of life she had become used to. Now that she was home again, unpacked and settled, the comfort of her old house and the presence of familiar objects filled her with confidence once more, and helped her regain her peace. Spring was in full swing, and the budding trees, the smell of flowers, and the pleasant warmth of the air all contributed to the renewal of a deep sense of elation and fulfillment.

Faint memories of the trial still lingered in her mind like clumps of weeds, but she had removed the unsightly ones. All that remained was a deep conviction that, on the stand in the chapel turned into courtroom, she had finally settled matters with Morrison: they were now, again, friends, and, if he had still been alive and single, she would have been glad to become his lover, although now, these many years after his death, such consummation could only be devoutly wished. Now it was *her* turn to dream, to reach in fantasy the very solace she had once denied.

That night she had taken a warm shower, dried herself, and combed and brushed her hair, so that it hung loose and smooth about her head. The water's warmth soothed her limbs and washed away her tiredness, replacing it with a dull, sensuous effervescence of the flesh, as if she'd been massaged by firm and knowing fingers. Conscious of a profound and very earthy joy and aware that such grace was transitory, she decided to indulge herself and relish every minute of it. She put on a clean nightgown, soft and silken and almost transparent, and, turning off the lights, walked slowly toward the bedroom window opened to the meadows bathed in the eerie light of a full moon. Standing in the center of the white sheet of light that streamed into the room, she closed her eyes, and, for a long moment, stretched, straining her face upwards, while, with both hands, she cupped her breasts, still full and youthful, though sagging in a tribute to her age.

The sensuous pose aided and enhanced her feelings of contentment, so that when she finally relaxed, turned around and got in her bed, she felt embraced and comforted by the sheets as if they were the arms of a gentle, tender lover lying at her side. Effortlessly, as she snuggled close to him in her imperishable fancy, her thoughts and feelings began to drift, becoming nameless, almost formless, and slowly blurred into fuzzy masses of warm colors. As she was about to fall asleep, the gossamer curtains at the window billowed inward, impelled by a soft, cool breeze that reached and caressed her face. She had not stirred at its touch, her face had shown no surprise, nor was her descent to restful slumber interrupted when, seconds later, for an instant, she vaguely thought she felt upon her languid, barely parted lips, the light, endearing pressure of her ghostly lover's goodnight kiss.

CHAPTER FOURTEEN

A couple of weeks later, Miss Carter found herself having lunch alone at the lobster place on the other side of the Kennebec River. Her mood was pensive, almost melancholic. She was bathed in some kind of indescribable feeling. Looking at the river sprawling in the distance and flowing toward the southwest, she recalled the times she had wished Morrison had been with her. In the past, she had been aware of a mixture of longing and resignation pervading such fantasies. It would have been nice to have Morrison with her, she felt, but she knew that could never be, for he was dead. There was also an element of sadness in the mixture, for she was keenly aware that she had let her friend die in ignorance of her love. There was a glint of shame in all this, as if she had been caught in an illicit act, though, in reality, her fault, if fault it was, lay in the fact that she had betrayed Morrison. She had assured him that nothing he said to her would undo her love for him—"care," that is—and then, when he confided in her, she had bolted from him like a frightened mare.

The feelings she experienced when she had lunch there by herself on summer afternoons, like this one, were complex and many-faceted, like reflections of the sun on the myriad movable mirrors that formed the surface of the river. But among them, on *this* day, was a special light that kept flashing now and then, never quite distinct, but impossible to overlook. It took many flashes before she really became aware of it. Something in her did not want to pay attention to it while, at the same time, another part of her was intently watching for it, as a cat waits for the next motion of a thread once its curiosity is piqued.

It took her some time before she realized that the intermittent light that made her blink was the memory of Jones. She was surprised, in a way, and yet not altogether, for since their first meeting Jones had assumed an important place in the gallery of her thoughts. For the most part, she reminisced about his ideas, the things he had said, the way he had said them, and their import for her. But today there was a new dimension appearing in the memories suddenly pullulating from the grounds of her subconscious. She was remembering *him*, not just his words or his ideas. It was his visage that came floating up to her, scintillating briefly while dancing amidst the silvery grays of her thoughts. And she became aware of a certain fondness attached to the vision, as if she yearned for his presence or wished to see him again, soon, almost as if she were waiting for him suddenly to appear. She knew, of course, that this was not likely, and yet she felt a kind of longing, a desire of the flesh for physical presence, for touch, for the confirmation of existence that only sensual closeness can bring. That's when she decided to write a letter to Jones.

. . . .

Jones had been surprised but pleased when he received her letter. He hadn't really expected to hear from her, but then again, the friendship that had developed between them was strong enough to support the promise of future encounters. He hadn't thought about initiating them—the idea simply hadn't occurred to him—but he was not at all averse to them getting to know each other better.

In the letter, she had thanked him for his attention while she had been in the city and assured him that she had thoroughly enjoyed herself in his company. She had expressed her gratitude once more for his willingness to hear her "confessions" (between quotation marks). She had talked a bit about the weather in Maine, about the flowers and the hills, and had ended by expressing the desire to hear from him at his leisure.

It took him some time to reply, for he was busy teaching summer school. But, toward the middle of the summer, he sat down to write to her. And for the first time, he was confronted by the fact that he didn't know what to tell her.

It wasn't that he had no news to relate, though, in fact, the little incidents of college life were scarcely important to someone not immediately involved. It was, rather, that he didn't know if that was what he should write about. He felt, somewhat apprehensively at first, that he would have to be more personal, that he would have to write about himself more than he had ever done to anyone (with the sole exception of the archbishop), and he wasn't sure he was ready for this. She, of course, had been infinitely more open, immeasurably more candid, especially after their second meeting. He felt he knew a lot more about her than she did about him, and he sensed that, if the friendship was to develop and grow, he would have to allow himself to be known; more, he would have to *make* himself known to her at least as much as she had made herself known to him. Friendship, as the old Latin saw had it, either finds the friends equal or makes them equal.

When he finally made time to write to Miss Carter, Jones realized, again for the first time, that the task would be even harder than he had initially surmised. As he began to write he became aware that there were feelings involved. To begin with, he couldn't decide how to address her. She had written, "Dear Mr. Jones," and she had always spoken to him in that manner, which conferred a degree of formality on their conversations, and she had signed herself, "Sincerely, Julie Carter." He couldn't remember ever having used her first name, an easy enough matter in conversation, but he couldn't very well avoid confronting the issue here, at the beginning of the letter. Calling her "Julie" implied a level of intimacy that he felt they hadn't achieved, and he was afraid of giving her cause for apprehension or of offending her. Finally, he settled on "Dear Miss Carter," hoping that matters would eventually clarify themselves and fall in place of their own accord. But as he began to write, he promised himself that he would end the letter, "Sincerely, Jim." This would somehow rectify matters if he had been too formal, and, at the same time, leave a nice, friendly aftertaste, like a cordial after an ordinary meal.

All this made Jones realize that he wasn't simply replying to Miss Carter's letter as he would have written to a colleague or a former student. No, there was something peculiar stirring inside him that made his thoughts flow differently. He was aware that he was imbuing his words with a certain ardor, unusual for him, which he wanted felt but not seen, and that he hoped would be detected without his making it too explicit. After all, he really didn't know what Miss Carter thought of him and whether or not she had any feelings for him deeper than those of gratitude for a bit of companionship enjoyed in a few brief encounters. The thought did occur to him that perhaps Miss Carter had experienced the same difficulties writing to him that he was living through now and that perhaps her words carried a heavier burden of feeling than had been initially apparent to him. He re-read her letter with this thought in mind, but hadn't detected any special sentiments or innuendos. Finally, he finished the letter and mailed it to Miss Carter, secretly hoping that she would reply soon, but still unwilling to admit this expectation to himself.

He didn't have to wait long. Miss Carter's letter came within a week, and its arrival stirred in him feelings of apprehension and desire to which he was most unfamiliar. The letter was still addressed to "Mr. Jones," but its contents were very personal, as her face-to-face communications had been, and its tone was friendlier than he had dared to expect.

After the initial greetings and expressions of delight and gratitude for his letter, Miss Carter returned to the subject that had brought them together in the first place—the question of Morrison. The letter contained no new facts, but in it Miss Carter expressed feelings that she hadn't acknowledged before, at least not to Jones. Referring to her friendship with Morrison, she had written:

> "We spend so much time closing ourselves to people that, when we really want to open up to someone special, we have to break down a brick wall rather than just open a curtain. It may have been that I had my heart's desire then, but I didn't realize it. Another time, I thought I had it when, in fact, I didn't. But too many years had passed before I noticed this. As I told you the second time we met, I don't want to repeat either error. I want to follow my heart's desire, what truly gives me bliss."

She hadn't elaborated, but the door she had left open proved too tantalizing for Jones to ignore, so he walked through it (not without apprehension), and, in his reply, he asked her to be more specific about what she meant.

Her next letter was brief. But in it, Miss Carter explained in greater detail what she meant by the pursuit of bliss.

> "Most of us desire what we know, what we have seen others desire. We see them fulfilled and wish in our hearts to be as happy as they are or seem to be. But in doing this, we are simply imitating others and their pursuits and conforming our desires to theirs. I've done this, too, because the temptation to be like everybody else is great. There is a kind of safety in treading where others have trod—you know, in traveling the more traveled road. But now I want to follow *my* heart's desire wherever it may lead, though where this might be, I don't yet know. I want to do what I have never done before: to turn from mirage to mystery and find happiness in the adventure."

Jones wrote back that he now had a better idea of what she meant. And he agreed with her. He, too, felt ready to explore at least some of the many possibilities that life still offered him. He could do this now, he said, because his life had become freer from distractions. "At some point," he remarked, "one's sight becomes un-blurred and then one sees one's goal clearly in focus." As he wrote this, he remembered what Morrison's widow had said about the poet, how, during the last years of his life, he had trailed himself like a hunter sighting his prey. "The un-blurring of one's sight frees desire, so that, like an arrow, it may seek its goal unerringly. If one is lucky," he added, "living is the slow un-blurring of one's sight, or, if you prefer, to live is to unfold desire slowly, freeing it from the obsession with things desired due to custom and social pressure, which it must transcend and ultimately leave behind."

Miss Carter's next letter had, again, been brief. She apologized for its brevity by claiming the need to prepare for the coming fall and winter, something that always entailed work around the house and the yard.

She continued the discussion of needs and desire, and she quoted a saying of Saint Francis of Assisi, which she wondered if Jones knew (he did): "I need very little, and the little I need, I need very little." She added, "To arrive at such point is one of my most important tasks."

Then she veered completely from this subject and asked Jones to write about his studies and his life as an academic. She explained that she wanted to get to know him better, so that their friendship could grow, and she assured him that she would reciprocate in future letters.

Jones felt a bit uncomfortable about this request, but he decided to comply, promising to himself to be merely factual and objective, but knowing deep down that he was deluding himself in pretending he could suppress or contain the feelings that had already begun to stir in him.

> "I found physics fascinating," he wrote, "but lacked the mathematical sophistication needed to do the problems and pass the tests. My understanding was purely conceptual. For instance, I *understood* that light travels in a curve and that, therefore, as my professor put it, if one looks into the distance for a sufficiently long period of time, one will eventually see the back of one's head. Yet I was more interested in what this fact meant *for life* than I was in passing tests on it. The curvilinear path of light from the eyes to the back of the head became for me a metaphor of solipsism, an image of the person who fails to relate to others—at least to *one* other. Magritte's painting of the man looking at the back of his head in a mirror became for me a picture of hell more terrifying than any burning cauldron—worse, even, than the 'sweating selves' of Bernanos."

This would have been all right as an objective description of his interests, but he hadn't been able to stop there.

> "And yet, at least a part or dimension of my life has been lived in an excruciating narrowness, so that I began to believe at some point that happiness was beyond my reach—at least that happiness which involves closeness with and transparency to another."

He had written all this with full awareness, and yet almost against himself, for he felt he was losing control of his feelings, that he was becoming defenseless against desires he had kept at bay for more than half a century. Little did he know that five hundred miles away, Miss Carter was fighting a similar battle with herself.

. . . .

Miss Carter didn't reply immediately to his last letter. In fact, several weeks passed, and the fall term was well under way when he finally received a longish letter from her. He had become fearful that he had offended her in some manner—perhaps by being too explicit about his feelings—though he tried to reassure himself that there was nothing in his words to offend her. At any rate, she must have gotten over whatever it was, for here, at last, he had a letter from her in his hands.

This letter was addressed to "Jim," not "Mr. Jones." That in itself made his heart skip a beat. He pored over the letter, reading it again and again, finding new meanings each time, wondering if he would ever understand it all, and pondering retorts and comments he would want to make when he wrote back.

After the usual pleasantries, Miss Carter launched into a fairly detailed narrative of her past, not the artistic one he knew well, since it was a matter of public record, but her teenage years and her sojourn in college. She concluded with a review of the current state of her feelings.

Her youth through high school had been peaceful and promising, she wrote, and she had moved on to college full of dreams and expectations. The new freedoms she found there had mesmerized her at the beginning, and had even interfered with her studies. In college she had gone through a couple of "infatuations," and, during the early years of her film career, she had "survived," she said, one brief, passionate sexual fling. Nothing had come of it, but an enduring doubt about her capacity to love remained, a doubt that was exacerbated after her break-up with Morrison. After this, she had withdrawn into herself, retaining only distant friendships from which she perceived no threat.

She didn't know, she wrote, whether she had ever been "in love," though she suspected, as she had said to Jones earlier, that perhaps she had been, albeit unaware of what it meant to be in love, or, perhaps, unaware of what it felt like to truly love some-one. Once, during a filming session, one of the actors, who was also a social acquaintance, had injured himself and had dropped to the floor at her feet, writhing in pain. Instead of bending to assuage his pain and offer a nurturing hand, she had stifled in herself the common human signs of compassion, stood unflinch-ing as a stolid witness to her friend's misery, and left all present, including herself, wondering whether she was truly capable of even the most elemental human sympathy.

She thought, too, that there was an element of wild rebel-lion, even of anarchy, in her unwillingness—or was it inabil-ity—to love. She wondered if she had felt that loving another entailed submission, something she would never be ready to concede. Or perhaps it was that she had been afraid of loving, of losing herself in passion. Again, perhaps she had been wary of being loved, of becoming indebted to someone because of love received—of feeling an obligation to reciprocate another's love, making her love merely part of a contract and not, therefore, something truly and generously given. She didn't know for sure, but she had thought a lot about these things, especially after ending her friendship with Morrison. This sad event was still surrounded by mystery, she said. Even now, at least some aspects of it remained beyond her comprehension.

She had also puzzled about her own sexuality. She didn't think of herself as prudish—after all, she *had* had a sexual affair—but she couldn't understand why the yearning for the pleasures of love-making had never overwhelmed her to the point of enticing her into relationships. From this perspective, again, she had been unable to understand her rejection of Morrison. Why had she felt threatened—if that was what she had felt—by Morrison's sexual fantasies? What had she found alarming in the dreams of erotic love contained in Morrison's poems? Wouldn't she have surrendered to passion with a man in an exchange of mutual love, had the opportunity presented itself, or was she fooling herself? How could she have suspected Morrison of sexual intentions without her own desires being betrayed, somehow, by her very claim? How could she have accused him of *anything*; he who would have died rather than hurt her, and who thought he loved her more than anyone ever had?

All this had led her to doubt her own sexual orientation, for even though she had enjoyed her carnal fling, it proved only that she could be erotically aroused by a man, nothing more. After all, many people dated and married in the pursuit of the usual, only to find out they had deluded themselves, forestalling for a while the painful and ineluctable (but also freeing) revelation. Perhaps the long and dreary solitude of her middle years was the result of an unwillingness to accept what seemed so evident: a desperate desire to resist what appeared inevitable and cling forlornly to what she would have wanted to be. On this matter, she had tortured herself mercilessly to extract a confession, but the truth still eluded her. Her unusually strong revulsion from Morrison might indicate that her suspicion was well founded, yet she had not been able to acquiesce and find peace in such a conclusion, and this, itself, had been a major source of both the pain of her isolation and her hope.

Her letter came to an end with a heart-rending outpouring of regret mixed, however subtly, with an acknowledged love for the poet and—here Jones's heart nearly exploded—an avowal of her love for *him*, Jones.

> "Bill, really, was a part of my life, and losing him brought me back to my original solitude, the one in which we are all born. I can't bring Bill back to life, but I refuse to go alone and unloved into the grave. I know what my heart desires, and that is to share the life left me intimately with another.

> Jim, I long for *you* to make me un-alone again and walk with me the last stages of my dearest and longest dream."

And that had been that.

. . . .

It took Jones several weeks to recover from the impact of Miss Carter's words. There was a great deal there for him to think over and assimilate. He realized what she was asking of him, and he had to ponder carefully, as he did just about everything, how to answer her and what the implications of his answer would be.

Jones had never been married. When he was fifteen, he had fallen head over heels for a high school girl two years older than he. They had enjoyed a lot of kissing and heavy petting, and one day, while his parents were at work, they had cut classes and gone to his home, titillated by the prospect of pleasures not yet experienced, enhanced beyond measure by the secrecy of it all. Once there they had caressed, kissed, and touched each other with great gratification. As their passion grew, they had undressed hurriedly, excited by the imminence of sexual consummation, and tumbled on his bed, twined and twisting into ever more pleasurable positions, straining for the ultimate that they knew was promised them. But as they thrust their young and eager bodies rhythmically against each other, reaching toward the climax of their love, he exploded in a prolonged and uncontrolled release of sexual passion, and he had suddenly become conscious of his role as pleasure giver. He had felt inadequate and doubted the truth of his partner's ringing surfeit. He had said nothing to her as they lay for a long time embraced together on the bed, but from that moment of doubt, their ardors had cooled. There had been no repetition of their lark. A couple of years later, he joined the seminary, and even though he had left to embark on an academic career, he had remained alone and uncommitted, with only one close friend: the archbishop. His teaching had become his "thing," as he had written to Miss Carter, adding, with a shade of self-criticism and perhaps to avoid the appearance of selfishness, that "there is a great deal of self-forgetfulness involved in absorption in work." He had concluded by telling Miss Carter that he felt ready "to begin anew," as he put it, as long as they walked side by side and provided he could always look into her eyes. Her eyes, he told her, as Dante had told Beatrice, were the only thing that brought peace to his desire.

Miss Carter wrote back delighted with his revelation. She reassured him, insisting that she understood his insecurities, which she shared. She said she felt encouraged by his willingness to respond and by the fact that he didn't seem at all threatened by the new possibilities opening up for them. Toward the end of her letter, she wondered if he really loved her and whether he was ready to pursue their friendship wherever it might lead.

He replied that he did, and that, if she was patient with him, he was willing to work strenuously at forging the wondrous ring of their love.

> "I've read somewhere that, in the encounter with God, the ethical is annulled because the ethical is a human construct and all constructs evaporate like puddles in the heat of the unforgiving sun of godhood. However that may be, I have yearned for such a total encounter with another of my kind as would cause a new and singular ethic to emerge out of the words uttered and received, just as the world emerged from God's words on that primordial dawn of all. I look forward to creating a new world with you."

. . . .

Toward Christmas, she sent him a card with his name scribbled all over it, wishing him the merriest, the happiest, the jolliest, the holiest holiday ever and wondering if he would have some time to come visit her. Clearly, his name had become for her like an incantation powerful enough to break the grip that loneliness had held around her heart. She knew she couldn't be saved alone, and he had come to realize the same. From then on their paths would never diverge.

Jones had been unable to drive up to Maine to spend some time with Miss Carter, but their correspondence had continued unabated. After so many years of solitary living, they felt they had to live through each other's backgrounds; they had to walk in each other's shoes, utter each other's favorite words, in order to arrive at a common language, a language uniquely their own. They had to grope through the dark alleys of memory in order to recover what was salvageable and could be used to shape a new present together. They were like masons constructing new edifices out of the ruins. A major part of such an effort consists in discarding obsolete and useless shapes while preserving what can add beauty and efficacy to the new structure.

In a sense, they were taking off their masks, shedding their costumes and the repertoire of language and behaviors accumulated since childhood. In the process, they came to see such trappings as impediments. People strained so much to cover up their nakedness, and yet it was this nakedness alone that symbolized the human essence. Perhaps this was the reason why the nude was such a favorite topic in art. Once all the uselessness of custom and taboo was gone, what remained was the naked suchness of each self, the liveliness by which they were, each and all, indistinguishably alive. Once this moment was reached, the stage was set for the beginning of a life together.

Not that this was the end. Rather, living together could only be the beginning of the final ascent toward the most rarefied heights attainable by any earnest seeker, growing closer to each other without surrendering their uniqueness and reaching for union while avoiding confusion and lack of distinction. Months later, in a book by Katherine Anne Porter, Jones had come across a passage that had brought to his mind this stage of their relationship. It spoke of "surrendering gracefully with an air of pure disinterestedness as much of your living self as you can spare without incurring total extinction." That was, precisely, what they were striving to achieve.

It was this starting point that Miss Carter and Jones had approached as winter had given way to spring, and the new buds announced the beginning of a new cycle of life.

CHAPTER FIFTEEN

Up to this point, Miss Carter and Jones had been like two convicts in adjoining cells who communicated by tapping on the wall. However, the time was coming for them to be released from their epistolary constraints. What would they say on the day of their deliverance, when meeting face to face for the first time since their avowals of love? What would they do?

Jones had decided to drive up to Waterville for spring vacation. Miss Carter had been delighted. And even though they both had apprehensions about this meeting, they kept these to themselves, dwelling, rather, on the positive side of things and promising themselves a wonderful time together.

Jones made the usual motel reservation and drove up to Maine, leaving as early as he could. The weather had been cold and rainy all through the northeast, and this slowed down his progress, so that he didn't get to Waterville until quite late. He checked in at the motel, and, as soon as he had settled in his room, he phoned Miss Carter to tell her that he had arrived safely, and that he would see her in the morning.

"As early as possible, Jim," she said. "I'm so eager to see you again!"

"I'll be there as early as I can," he promised, adding, "I'm sorry I didn't get here early enough to see you today."

"At least you're here," she replied, and then added: "Oh, Jim, it's so nice to know you are near!"

"I'm glad, too," he answered. Then, "Julie, have a good night's sleep. I love you. I'll see you in the morning."

"I love you too, Jim," she said softly, almost like a whisper.

Jones went to the restaurant in search of some food, but the place was closing. After some pleading, they served him a cup of soup and some crackers, which he consumed hurriedly, not wanting to inconvenience the staff further.

Back in his room, Jones undressed, put on his pajamas, brushed his teeth, and settled down comfortably in one of the chairs. He began to read a book he had brought with him, *Sex and the Mystical Path*, and had barely read a couple of pages when he realized that he would not be able to keep awake for long. Still, he read on. The words, "We love each other, but which of us is which?" intrigued him, and he was pondering them when he gently floated off into sleep. His own heavy breathing awoke him after a while, and he read some more, making an effort to keep awake and simultaneously comprehend a fascinating passage in which the author was describing the intimate union between two lovers:

> The ellipse, as the ancients taught, is a profound symbol of the union brought about by true love. For, as Modicus says in his *Geometria Mystica Conjugalis* [1379], "the ellipse

> is a geometrical figure resulting from the overlapping of two independent circles, involving an interpenetration or coinherence of the two, so that the lovers, being two and independent, merge into each other to form a new reality in the world." Such a symbol, too, was the original human described by Plato in his *Symposium*, male and female fashioned into the perfection of a sphere, androgyne and hermaphrodite at once, a creature marvelous in strength, wisdom, and even running speed, a being so powerful that the gods feared it would usurp their power, and therefore had sundered it—

He dozed off again, and, when he woke, decided to give up on reading. Putting the book away, he turned on the TV and flipped through the programs, eventually choosing a "Galaxy" re-run.

He must have dozed off yet again, for when he woke up with a mild sensation of discomfort in his bent neck, the show was over, and the news was on. He tried to watch, but found himself closing his eyes and drifting into semi-consciousness, so he decided to give in to sleep and retire for the night.

He was almost asleep, when the phone rang, startling him somewhat. He picked up the receiver and said, "Hello."

"Jim?" inquired Miss Carter on the other end. "Is that you?"

"Yes, Julie," Jones replied, raising himself a little on his elbow. "Is everything all right?"

"Yes, of course," she answered. After a moment's hesitation, as if gathering her courage, she asked, "Jim . . . may I come over?"

"Er . . . sure," he said. He wasn't prepared for that, but he didn't know what else to say. "I was in bed already," he added as an afterthought. He didn't wish to prevent her coming over, but he wanted her to know his situation.

"It's all right," she replied. "I'll be right over."

He got out of bed and turned on the lights. He had brought no robe with him, and he didn't feel like putting on his clothes again, so he decided he would receive her in his pajamas.

Sitting down on a chair to wait for Miss Carter, he must have dozed off, for the next thing he knew was that someone was knocking at the door. He opened it and let Miss Carter in, closing the door after her. She placed a small bag she was carrying on a chair, and then quickly turned to him.

"You look cute in your pajamas," she said, tapping his arm and smiling slightly, with a hint of unease in her voice.

"Oh, well," he replied, a bit embarrassed. Then, looking at her, he asked, "What's the matter? Are you upset?"

"No, not at all. Jim," she said, drawing close to him, taking his hands in hers, and looking at him straight in the eye, "let's sleep together. We don't have much time left, you and me. If we want to move toward a closer union, we have to start living it."

"I know," he said, "but—"

"Jim," she interrupted, placing her right index finger on his lips, "we love each other. We shouldn't deny each other the warmth of our ageing bodies."

"You're right," he concurred, relaxing a little.

"It's a matter of love," she reassured him, grasping his hands again. "For us, it's a matter of love. Love will lead the way eventually to . . . other things."

"I know," he said. Then, with a certain pedantry, he added, "Who would give rules to lovers?"

"Who said that?" she inquired, holding him at arm's length.

"I did," he answered.

"*You* didn't write that," she said with a laugh, "*who* did?"

"Boëthius," he replied, smiling at her, "but it's as true as if I had written it myself, even if I say so."

"Yes," she said softly, straining upward against his body, searching for his lips.

He put his arms around her, and she crossed hers around his neck. They kissed gently at first, then more passionately, venting some of the accumulated yearnings of years. Then they stopped, almost reluctantly, unsure how to proceed. And to mask their indecision, they began to get ready for bed. He puffed up the pillows while she picked up the small bag she had brought and went to the bathroom to change. After a few minutes, she came back to the room wearing a silken, almost transparent, negligee and carrying in her hand a peignoir that she placed upon a chair. While she was getting in bed, he switched off the lights and then got in next to her.

For a while they lay there quietly, each to one side of the bed, expectant yet uncertain, like latecomers at a party wondering what to do next.

"Come close to me," she said as she turned toward him. "Hold me. Let me lay my head on your chest."

He hugged her as she rested her head on his chest, her arms around him, her right leg straddled over his.

"I love you, Jim," she said, after a while.

The words had slipped out of her mouth almost without her noticing it. It was the first time in years she had proclaimed her love to someone face to face. She was surprised, but not upset. In fact, she felt somewhat elated, pleased with herself, for the affection she felt for Jones proved she could love, after all.

"I love you too," he replied softly, rubbing her shoulder gently. "I love you very much."

They remained that way for a long time, getting increasingly comfortable with each other. The memory of Morrison flickered briefly and barely noticeably in their minds like the sputtering of a wick drowning in an excess of molten wax. In their different ways, their lives had become inextricably linked to the poet's, catapulting both of them beyond themselves and to the brink of fulfilling the poet's fancies.

Their fleeting remembrance of Morrison, unstated though it remained, stirred in them a faint feeling of regret, like the bitter taste of lime. It was the sincere sadness for what could have been, but it was tempered by the recognition that in their love they were realizing the poet's hope. Slowly, drowsiness overtook them, and they surrendered willingly to its sway. They felt peaceful and contented, for they knew they were safe in each other's arms. They had taken another step in their journey toward each other and toward the fullness of their love. After a while, their measured breathing gave proof to the guardian spirits of the night that they were asleep.

. . . .

The rain had not cleared when they got up the next morning. It felt damp and chilly.

The morning was half gone, so they decided to go back to the house to have brunch. After fixing the food for themselves, they sat down at the table by the long window, looking out onto the open fields, which looked desolate in the falling rain.

"I hope I didn't upset you last night," Miss Carter said, though her statement was really a question.

"Why do you ask?"

"I sensed some unease," she replied. "I forgot you're Catholic, but I didn't mean to offend you or entice you to anything you might not have wanted to do."

"Quit worrying," he said, reaching for her hand and holding it affectionately. "My only source of unease is my insecurity. I'd hate not to be able to please you."

"I understand," she said, retrieving her hand. She picked up her cup of coffee with both hands and turned toward the window. After a sip or two, she added, "You know, we have never talked about sex."

"What is there to talk about?" he inquired. "I have never had problems with sex."

"Because you have hardly had any," she quipped delightedly, looking at him and laughing. "Sorry, I just couldn't help that," she said, as her laughter abated.

"That's all right," he rejoined. "Really, I have never seen evil in sexuality. Perhaps because I never had a problem with pleasure, whether sexual or otherwise. All the traditional objections seemed to me to be misguided really, the product of what today we would call abnormal minds." He stopped for a moment, weighing his words. "Perhaps that's too strong a term. Perhaps *unbalanced* is better."

"Even Saint Augustine?"

"Yes. You see, having enjoyed sexual pleasure, he had to justify giving it up, and the easiest way was to condemn it as evil. We all do that. When we choose between alternatives, we always damn the one not chosen in order to minimize the anguish we would feel were the other alternative prove to be the better one. Psychologists call this *cognitive dissonance*," he said, tracing quotation marks in the air with his fingers. "We can't live with too much dissonance, and calling one alternative *evil* makes the chosen one seem better. The problem is that Augustine's choice, and his damning of sexual pleasure, were taken as *the* truth and imposed upon all believers. Christians have had trouble understanding that pleasure can be part of love—not just of receiving, but of *giving* love."

"I agree," she said. "I simply didn't know what you felt, Jim, and I wanted to make sure—"

"It's that people have a weird view of love," Jones interrupted her, "even of sexual love. Even those who think that sex is good but that it must be kept in check can think only of control or of abstinence. They can only think of giving up things. It never occurs to them that using things rightly *is* a form of control . . . that there is an asceticism of right use, if you see what I mean."

"Go on," she said, encouraging him.

"Giving pleasure to someone, being generous in the experience of pleasure, requires as much—or even more—self-control than giving up pleasure altogether. Knowing how to use sex, knowing how to love in and through sex, is one of the hardest ascetical disciplines anyone can practice. Celibates know nothing of this," he added, "for their asceticism is one of renunciation, but for couples, this is the path toward holiness."

"Have you ever written about this, Jim?" she inquired. "This is a beautiful thought."

"No, I never thought I could, being single. Who would take me seriously?"

"I would have," she said.

"Ah, Julie dear, now can you see why you had no reason to be apprehensive about my feelings?" He looked into her eyes for signs of understanding and approval. "You have created for us both this possibility, this chance of using our sexuality as a stairway to heaven, of moving toward union and oneness in love by giving each other pleasure. It's not sex that would bother me, but not being able to give you pleasure, to not be able to love you more and more through the very ecstasies of love-making."

"Until we become one flesh?" she added, half as question, half as statement.

"Yes, until we become one flesh . . . and even more."

"Even more?"

"Yes, even more," he repeated, with a certain emphasis. "The carnal oneness achieved in intercourse is a *mystery*," he said, again gesturing the quotation marks around the word.

"Saint Paul said that. That means that it's a symbol, a symbol of the union of God and world. Or of soul and world for the Stoics. Intercourse is a sacrament of the unity of the world. Ah, Julie, to be able to experience *that*!"

"We will, Jim," she said to him, reassuringly, reaching for his hand and holding it firmly, lovingly. "We will. We have some way to go, you and I, before we sacramentalize the world. That's why I thought we should get started soon."

"You are the wise one," he said.

With that he got up and walked behind Miss Carter's chair. He placed his hands lovingly on her shoulders, and the two of them remained there for a while, looking out the window, where the rain was still falling unremittingly.

. . . .

During Jones's stay in Waterville, he and Miss Carter continued to sleep together. They slept in the motel, for there the bed was bigger. They carried on their kissing and began, discreetly at first, exploring each other's bodies. In all this they let themselves be guided by their deep and tender love. The days were times of quiet conversation; the nights, of sensuousness and bliss.

One night, toward the middle of the week, they shed their night clothes and embraced in the darkness of the room. Delicately, with patience and tact, they explored each other's bodies, seeking and giving pleasure equally, guiding each other through the intricate maneuvers of love. Eventually, her caresses and his passion enabled him to sustain her, and she rode him with abandon, galloping in a nocturnal charge against the hordes of lonelinesses past, triumphant now, and forever un-alone. He had understood, and, when his moment came, he joined with her in an exultant paroxysm of love and unity regained. From that night on they would be inseparably one.

CHAPTER SIXTEEN

Upon his return from Waterville, Jones took stock of his situation. It was clear that he and Miss Carter had been falling in love over a period of years. It was clear, too, that they had traversed successfully the domains of background and achievement that separated them. Through their correspondence, they had striven to know each other as well as any two human beings could, and they had begun to incorporate into one single point of view as many of their separate opinions, biases, and idiosyncrasies as possible. The goal was to become of one mind while becoming one flesh. Becoming one soul, the task that still lay ahead, could only take place if mind and body were perfectly unified. Building one soul from two disparate lives was like forging a sword: the alloys had to be melted, the dross discarded, the purified metal hammered into shape, heated once more, and finally tempered by immersion in cold water. The only difference was that here they were the forgers of themselves, and the purgation involved their dear selves. It was up to them whether they became cheap, dull swords or glittering blades of the finest steel.

It didn't take Jones much time to realize that these efforts would consume time, a commodity of which they couldn't promise themselves a great deal. They would have to spend much time together talking and traveling, exploring themselves and the world they were now approaching jointly. It didn't seem possible that he could continue to teach while giving to their relationship the time and energy it demanded.

Because of these considerations, he decided to hand in his resignation at the university. He would finish the term, of course, but this would be his last semester of teaching. He would put an end to a career that spanned four decades, but he would not "retire," as the expression went, for what he was doing was gathering his energies like a jumper in order to reach new heights.

Once he arrived at his decision, he communicated it to Miss Carter, who wrote back immediately, concurring with him and looking forward with great anticipation to joint travels and adventures. He also telephoned his friend the archbishop and arranged to meet him in his office at the chancery.

On the appointed day, Jones was ushered into the archbishop's spacious office, and he greeted his friend with the usual effusion. After a few pleasantries, he explained to the archbishop the purpose of his visit. He wanted to bring him up to date on what was going on in his life, especially as it concerned Miss Carter.

"We have been writing to each other," he offered, "and we have just spent some time together in Maine. During spring vacation, you know," he added, not wanting to give the impression that he was neglecting his duties.

"I wish I could take a vacation myself," the archbishop said, noncommittally. "It must have been beautiful up there at this time."

Jones decided to be straightforward. He talked to his friend about his new-found love and about the direction his relationship with Miss Carter was taking. He had felt a twang of embarrassment when mentioning the sexual aspect of the relationship, so he had not gone into it in any detail, but had merely referred to it as if in passing, or as an afterthought, and in the context of their spiritual development. What he had wanted to know, he had said, was whether or not they were on the right spiritual path. From his brief years in seminary, he remembered that it wasn't always easy to discern the right path from the wrong one, and that many mistakes were made because the wrong appeared right. A detour can begin as a nicer looking road than the straight thoroughfare, and the luring shorter, steeper steps do not always lead to the desired heights.

"So, you're in love?" his grace asked with a smile.

"You could say that," Jones answered, "but somehow that doesn't do justice to what I feel or to what I am experiencing."

"I can understand that," the archbishop replied.

Jones wanted to ask his friend why he felt he could understand, when he had never been in love with a woman, but he refrained.

"At our age," Jones said, wagging a finger at the archbishop, "we have to look carefully where we walk. We can't afford mistakes and side roads because we can't promise ourselves the time needed to get back on course. Tell me—"

"You were always the wise one," the archbishop interrupted.

"This is not a matter of wisdom, but of prudence," Jones insisted. "What do you think?"

The archbishop spoke to him reassuringly, reminding him that the ardors of love could be purifying, like the furnace fires that burn away the dark dross of the gold, and that Jones himself had once remarked that Elijah the prophet had been whisked to heaven in a chariot of fire.

"I remember that," Jones said, smiling, and punctuating each word for emphasis. He leaned back and looked up and around as if relishing the recollection. "I was so frustrated with the trend of his interrogation that I had to come up with something to shake him up. I don't think it made a bit of difference to him, but I felt better!"

"I did, too," the archbishop concurred. "Jim, there isn't much I can tell you that you don't already know. Just a reminder: Watch carefully the movements of your soul. If they are peaceful and noiseless, like a drop of water falling on a sponge, take them as inspiring and conducive to further progress, but if they are harsh and noisy, like water splashing on a stone, beware and reconsider."

That seemed to put an end to their conversation. Jones got up and looked for a moment into the eyes of his old friend.

"You will pray for me—for us—won't you?" he asked.

"You are beyond my prayers," the archbishop replied, quietly. "I just hope I move closer to the summit with the same purity of heart."

"Is it easier alone, John?"

"I don't know." Looking away, the archbishop continued, "Kierkegaard thought it was the only way, and so did Plotinus." His voice trailed off, and he sighed deeply before adding, slowly at first, then more evenly, "As I heard you talk today, I felt a pang of sadness, as if we were bidding each other farewell, but I told myself I wasn't being left alone, because you and I have moved through life together in friendship. I feel sure, somehow, that you are still my friend."

"Always," Jones said firmly, as he took his leave.

. . . .

In the middle of June, Jones and Miss Carter rented a small condominium in the Outer Banks of North Carolina. It was located in an old development named Pelican Watch, in Kitty Hawk. There they spent endless hours meditating, lulled by the rhythm of the waves, drawn into the mysteries of life, receding and advancing like the tides, but always constant, undiminished, inexhaustible. They had watched the sun rise over the ocean while dolphins cavorted in the surf, and they had seen it set over the land in the horizon, while sitting peacefully in a chapel they had discovered in the middle of the swampy brush.

During their warm sojourn by the sea, their senses reawakened from the long torpor that years of lone living had induced in them. Jones's condition was by far the worst, for, in the city, sensory stimuli must be warded off in order to survive. And after years of building ramparts, one no longer notices one is immured. Stimuli are so plentiful, and they impinge on people so insistently, so inopportunely, that their very multitude becomes a threat rather than an enrichment, and they float away wasted, like the surging waters of a typhoon rushing upon parched land without drenching it. Living in a little town where life transpired languidly, even on the most hectic days, on the other hand, Miss Carter had enjoyed more opportunity to savor the exquisite morsels of experience that rural Maine could serve to connoisseurs. And yet both of them were in need of lessons—so much of life dulls the senses, especially the insistence on the logic of things, but also the demeaning of play, the suspicion of touching, and the despising of hands-on learning.

In Kitty Hawk, during the warm days and often sultry nights, they rediscovered the simple facts of life. Away from deodorants, perfumes, and insecticides, they became aware again that *everything* in the world smells. They relished again, as if for the first time, the odor of freshly mown grass, earth wet by the summer rains, sea breezes, and seagulls' nests. They came to know their own smells, individual as a fingerprint, and to relish them intimately as they seeped through cilia, neurons, and nerves into their own brains. Miss Carter remembered how each of her movie-lovers had smelled, and she thought that she might still be able to identify each by his natural scent. In turn, Jones also recalled the delightful odor of acetone which, as a child, he had used as solvent in order to make his own model airplane glue.

Basking in the sun, relishing the texture as they wriggled their toes in the wet sand, and, especially, holding hands, caressing and massaging each other, they had become sensitized again to the power of touch. For the first time, Jones had really comprehended the meaning of that passage from Lucretius he had read so often that he could quote it from memory:

> For touch,
> Touch, ye holy powers of God,
> Is the feeling of the body; whether it be
> When something from without makes its way in,
> Or when a thing which in the body had birth
> Hurts it, or gives it pleasure as it issues forth,
> The life-engendering deed of Venus to perform.

As the days and nights passed, they came to agree with Freud that the whole body is an erogenous zone, as they did with the old Zen seers who said no wisdom is possible without enhancing the role of the senses. To commune with the world, even with the God who created it and dwelled in it in spirit and in truth, requires that a person sense it in all its multiplicity, through all the diversity of the human sensorium. Christian asceticism had been mistaken in this, for what was necessary was not renunciation but refinement, sharpening the acuity of hearing and sight, relishing all tastes and smells, and rendering one's skin transparent to the universe. The point was not to silence the multitude of noises as if they were impediments, but to muster them into one colossal, polyphonic, and sonorous symphony.

. . . .

They then traveled to India, to the Taj Mahal, that poem in white marble that Shah Jahan had spoken to his dead queen, Mumtaz. They spent hours sitting on the cool floor in the lower tomb, where the remains of the lovers were interred, meditating on the strength of love that can transcend death and that, indeed, can soar beyond the reach of mind to rest in the bosom of Allah.

On their way back, they stopped in Florence, where nine-year-old Dante had first experienced *la vita nuova*, for, like him, they felt possessed by a "new god" stronger than any they had yet worshiped, and more demanding, for it exercised full mastery over their lives.

From there they proceeded to Austria, where they had rented a small cottage in the Alps, near the Haus zum Regenbogen. They planned to spend several weeks there, giving themselves to meditation in a context as devoid of distractions as could possibly be devised.

The first morning after their arrival, they got up late—the sun was already up, and its brilliant light made the morning air almost scintillate with brightness. The snows on the high peaks of the sierra shone starkly against the blackness of the exposed, jagged rocks that thrust themselves upward as if the earth were straining for the sky in one last orgasmic surge. The sky was light blue, with that special tinge it assumes high up in the mountains: a depthless hue that hints at the interminable nature of its reach. Jones noted, of course, that this was the color of her eyes, and he remembered how they had always seemed to hold an invitation to adventure. The air was brisk. Its chill came from the heights and not just as remnant of the night's cold. It felt fresh and pure, like something good and healthy and worthy to be breathed.

They dressed slowly, very much aware of each other's bodies, touching them every so often, occasionally caressing, kissing each other warmly but gently, striving in all this to maintain a mood of wonder and desire.

Eventually, they walked out onto the wooden deck that rose above the ground. They sat down comfortably on a bench, pushing very close to each other, and, for a while, they let their eyes wander slowly, gaze unfixed, taking in the panorama of rock, snow, and sky that spread before them. Then they closed their eyes and pondered more inwardly the secrets hidden by the mountains under a pall of snow. They thought about themselves and visualized lovingly the pleasures they desired and those they would like to give to each other as they created their world.

The sun was quite high in the sky when they arose from their meditation. They put their arms around each other's waists and walked thus together, gently, inside the cabin in search of sustenance for their hungry stomachs.

They didn't eat much—fried trout left over from another meal, toast, and a steaming cup of barley soup. After a stroll, they soon returned to the warm cottage. Lying down to rest on the couch, holding each other, they fell asleep. At some point they must have felt cold, for they pulled an Afghan on themselves.

They woke up from their nap in the middle of the afternoon. Walking out again onto the deck, they watched the changing shadows on the mountains around them and spied the clouds—flimsy and barely discernible in some places, thick and ominous in others—climbing slowly from the valleys below.

Back inside, they sat down comfortably at either end of the sofa and took turns reading aloud to each other from *The Hymns of Inanna*:

> Sister, come with me to my garden,
> come to my garden with me,
> to my orchard
> where I grow my apple tree,
> where I plant sweet honeyed seed.
> . . . .
> Last night as I, the Queen, was shining bright,
> as I, the Queen of Heav'n, was shining bright,
> as I shone bright and danced
> exalting at the coming of the night,
> he came to me;
> my Lord, the Shepherd, came to me.
> He clasped my hand,
> he brought his neck to mine,
> ready for my holy loins;
> the tall grasses in his field are ripe,
> and in his fullness I delight!
> . . . .
> He dragged both hands around my hips,
> he softened my thighs with oil,
> he stroked the grasses of my glen
> and parted them ready to plow.
> . . . .

By the time they finished, the sun was hiding behind the mountains. The sun set early here because of the height of the sierra, but its light endured for quite a while as it raced to its encounter with the sea. After they had eaten dinner, they sat for a while on the sofa, very close to each other, enjoying their closeness and their bodies' warmth, watching the evening draw close.

When dark finally descended, they went to their bedroom. They undressed in front of each other in a ritual that reversed the morning one, touching and caressing each other lovingly, almost worshipfully. They then lay in the center of the bed, she on her back and he, on her left, on his right side. She had raised her legs and he had gently swung his lower body around so that his hardened *linga* rested barely inside her *yoni*. She had then lowered her legs, placing them over his body, locking him up, thus, as he was stationed at her door. In this position, feeling restful and at ease, they remained for a long time, meditating on their love and the offering of their bodies to each other. It was thus, some Indian mystics preached, at the core of a most intimate and ineffable union, that the universe had been created, and every human act of intercourse, for those who could understand, replicated that first coital act, its climax weakly symbolized by the "Big Bang" that scientists speak about.

After a while he felt the sexual tension rise in him, and it culminated in a rapture in which he felt as if the whole world were being reborn, and they too with it, this time, however, at-one and forever intertwined.

Later on, sleep found them under the covers, huddled in each other's arms, breathing softly and rhythmically.

. . . .

They followed this routine for several days. At times, while they lay contentedly on their bed at night, she would enjoy the *rin no tan*, those specially weighted, metal, pleasure balls she could insert into herself, then rock back and forth, the moving balls inside her giving the thrusting, highly pleasurable feeling of intercourse. At times they would sit cross-legged on the bed, facing each other, centering their thoughts on each other's sex *chakras*, as if a magnet were drawing them there and holding them captive, and striving to feel the imaged, living flame of love as if it were being touched. After a while, they would synchronize each other's breathing rhythms while contracting and releasing the muscles of their sex *chakras*, until they felt the warmth of love rise within themselves and experienced themselves mystically united by a powerful current flowing out and into each other. After enjoying this state for as long as they could, they would kiss softly and give themselves to restful sleep.

They avoided distractions, striving to center their attention on themselves—not on their selves, really, but on the union they were forging which, as with the sculpting of a precious jewel, required the craftsman's utmost concentration. The conditions here were ideal for this degree of focus, allowing them to be present and available to each other all the time. They talked little. After all, their travels, their walks, their conversations, their tending to the necessities of food and sleep, and even their sexual explorations were all spiritual disciplines designed to bring them ever closer to their goal. The days they spent at the cabin in the Alps were like a mystical course that took them farther and higher than they had ever been before alone. Jones could only compare it with the conversation St. Augustine had held with his mother, Monica, at Ostia, shortly before her death, a conversation in which, as he put it, "they had raised themselves past themselves and all creation, and carried by their inward musing they had slightly touched the Mystery beyond."

One evening, as they were getting ready for bed, they felt drawn to each other by a stronger passion than usual. Their kisses and caresses had been more exquisitely delicate and prolonged, so that, when they finally lay in bed, their bodies and their souls hungered strongly for each other. He was on his back as she climbed on him, her body writhing, and her spirit moaning her unspeakable desire. Firm, erect, he was drawn into her womb, and both moved as nature had instructed them, clasping each other strongly, then frenetically as their climax neared, exploding then in uncontrolled release, bursting the limits of their egos, merging through each other with the powerful cosmic forces that pulsed in them. At that moment of ultimate enjoyment and unbelievable ecstasy, they understood what it meant to be *one flesh*—that their flesh was coextensive with the world, that they were made up of the same stuff as the stars, and that in their paroxysm of union, the cosmos itself was clashing with itself amorously as the sea's waves crash upon the rocks of the earth to which they both belong. They had come upon this shapeless view as though emerging from a cloud into the bright, limitless beyond, yet their realization was not a concept that they thought, but "an emotionally fringed awareness" that flooded their consciousness as water seeps through the beach's moistened sands. Moreover, the whole experience had been made possible by the long, arduous discipline through which they had lovingly progressed.

From that day on, their joy knew no limits. They still lived as separate individuals with all the quirky kinks they had developed all these years. But, without relinquishing them, they had transcended their selves and had brought to pass on earth the union that the sages speak about. This was, truly, yin and yang, except that they felt as if they were a circle that, rotating on itself, could show first this, then that aspect of itself. They knew, finally, that what each of them was would, from then on, be forever but an aspect of what they were together. Eternally, the glimpse of one would only be a partial vision of the whole.

And this, too, was the case with the universe. The union with themselves, in that magnificent paroxysm of love, had made them transparent to the world, the earth from which they had come after billions of years of evolution, the cosmos that they were, really, except that only at such exalted moments had they been able to see that they were the universe become conscious of and enamored with itself. This was the mystery—so simple, so sublime.

Review Requested:

If you loved this book, would you please provide a review at Amazon.com?

CPSIA information can be obtained at www.ICGtesting.com
Printed in the USA
BVOW04s0847060916

460953BV00001B/22/P